28.

The Sheriff of Red Rock

When Jake Helsby saw a rider heading into town he figured there would be trouble. It started at Fred Bennet's place, the Circle B, where somebody had put a piece of lead into Fred. One of the hands reckoned the Grissom kid was responsible but Jake suspected there might be more to it.

Why was the mayor so anxious to get a noose around the suspect's neck? And what was Lily Jeffords's interest in the kid's well being? Even as he searched for the true culprit, Jake had his own dark secret to protect.

The Sheriff of Red Rock

H. H. CODY

A Black Horse Western

ROBERT HALE · LONDON

ISBN-10: 0-7090-8141-3
ISBN-13: 978-0-7090-8141-8

Robert Hale Limited
Clerkenwell House
Clerkenwell Green
London EC1R 0HT

Typeset by
Derek Doyle & Associates, Shaw Heath
Printed and bound in Great Britain by
Antony Rowe Limited, Wiltshire

ONE

Jake Helsby knew there was going to be trouble the minute he saw the rider heading in the direction of Red Rock. Shading his eyes he took a good look at the man. Yeah, sure enough, it was Al Dawkins, a hand from the Circle B, the big spread up near the river.

Helsby hawked and spat into the dust. It had been too damned quiet in Red Rock for a while now. He took another look at the rider. It was going to take him a spell to get into town. He went back into the office where it was cool. No point frying, he reckoned.

Helsby sat back in his chair, and waited until he heard the pounding of hoofs in the dry street outside. He leaned forward and tried to look business-like. Sure enough, the door burst open and Al stumbled in. He was a big fella and the weather was treating him cruel. His fat face was covered with dust, sweat rolled through it. His gut heaved like it was a living thing. Helsby had often thought that Al's gut had a mind of its own.

Al flopped against the cabinet that the town council had bought for the sheriff's office. His mouth was wide open and his flabby lips were shaking like a leaf in a storm. Helsby got up. He took the scoop and put it in the pail of water by the desk. 'Take it easy, Al, git this inside you, it'll make you feel better.'

Helsby put his hand on Al's shoulder to steady him, and put the scoop to Al's lips. Al slurped the water down real quick, then wiped his mouth with the back of his hand.

'Thanks, Jake. You got to come down to the Circle B,' he gasped.

Helsby let go of Al, and refilled the scoop. Al was still shaking. Helsby fed him the water.

'What is it? Rustlers?'

Al wiped his mouth again. 'No, there's bin a shootin'.'

Helsby's eyes hardened. There hadn't been a shooting in Red Rock since he became sheriff.

'Who's bin shot?'

'The ol' man,' Al whispered.

The old man. Fred Bennet, who'd stolen the Circle B from the earth, and held it against rustlers, bad men, and anybody else who tried to take it from him. Al had calmed a mite.

'Any idea who did it?'

'The young Grissom kid. He was arguin' with

6

Fred yesterday afternoon. Reckon he shot him.'

'At the ranch?' Helsby asked, getting himself a scoop of water.

'No, out on the trail, by the front gate. Fred was playin' poker in the Lucky Lady. Fred played there every Friday night. Grissom knew that. He'd played there on Friday nights as well.'

'Don't mean Grissom shot him,' Helsby said, taking another scoop from the bucket.

'Don't mean he didn't,' Al replied, his breathing coming a mite easier.

'Better be gettin' out there,' Helsby said heading for the door.

Al looked at him. 'Ain't you forgettin' somethin'?'

Helsby looked at him.

'Yer gun.'

'Guessed there was somethin',' Helsby said, taking his rig down from the peg behind the door.

'How'd you git to be sheriff?' Al asked.

Helsby didn't like to think about that.

They headed out to the Circle B under a steadily strengthening sun. When they rode into the yard, most of the crew was gathered round a flat bed. From the way they were holding themselves, Helsby could see they were pretty het up.

He climbed down and tied his horse to the rail. The crew made way for him as he approached the wagon. Helsby pulled back the blanket they had covered Fred with.

'Bin shot in the back,' Les Moran, the foreman said.

Helsby could sense Moran's temperature going up.

Fred Bennet was about sixty. Nobody knew his real age. When Helsby came to think about it, nobody knew much about Fred, except that he was tough. Nobody knew where he came from when he had first come to Red Rock a good few years back. Nobody except his new attorney knew anything about his private affairs.

Behind him, the sheriff felt the impatience of the mob. Yes, it was a mob, not a ranch crew.

'We gonna get Grissom?' Moran asked him sharply.

Helsby turned on him. 'No we ain't gonna get him. I am.'

Moran didn't like it, and took a step forward. Helsby knew that this was it. If he backed off, the mob would go after Grissom, and they would lynch him for sure. Moran took another step forward. The two men were close up, too close for gunplay, Helsby figured, but he had to do something or there would be two dead men.

Him and Grissom.

Moran started to say something, but Helsby's fist sent him to the floor. The fella behind Moran picked him up.

'Anybody else want to come out to the Grissom

place?' Helsby asked them.

Nobody did.

Helsby rode to the Grissom place on his own. It was a small ranch, less than a quarter the size of the Circle B. It was a ranch that never quite got started. Young Grissom's grandpa had taken to rotgut whiskey before he took to hard work, and Grissom's pa hadn't been able to get it back. Now, there was just young Grissom and his ma, and half a dozen hands to keep the place from going under. The couple of hundred beeves they had weren't in such good shape.

Martha Grissom came to the door when Helsby hauled up.

'He in trouble agin, Jake?'

'Ain't rightly sure,' Helsby said, shaking his head. 'Fred Bennet's bin shot.'

'An' you came here, Jake, just to make yer job easier.'

'It's like I said. I don't rightly know. You gonna tell me where he is?'

For a second she thought about it, and Helsby thought she was going to tell him.

'No, Jake, I ain't gonna tell you where he is. I think yer a fair man, but he's my boy, an' I got to be sure. He's all I got left.'

Helsby sighed heavily. It was a day like he thought it might be. A day filled with trouble.

'Martha, just tell me where he is. I don't want to

9

see him git hurt, an' the way things are shapin' up over at the Circle B, he's likely to be in trouble. Dick would be better off in a cell,' Helsby said.

'No, Jake, find him if you can, but I won't help you.'

'You're makin' a mistake,' Helsby told her. 'Like I said I don't want to see him hurt, but if those Circle B boys go lookin' fer him an' find him, he might finish up hangin' from the nearest tree or with a bullet in him.'

'Sorry, Jake, but I've said my piece.'

'I'm sorry too, Martha. I don't want any more trouble than there has been, but I think there will be.'

Helsby mounted up with a bad feeling, and rode back to Red Rock. When he got there he could feel the change in the town, and guessed that word about the shooting had got round. He hauled up outside the office, and hitched his horse to the rail.

'Git him yet?' Moran shouted from the veranda of the saloon across the street.

Helsby turned to face him as he came off the veranda, with a beer in his hand, followed by a couple more men from the Circle B.

'Not yet,' Helsby said, preparing for trouble.

'Takin' yer time, ain't yer,' Moran said crossing the street.

'You might not have known it,' Helsby said, 'But I could lock you up fer bein' drunk on the

10

public street.'

'So lock me up,' Moran said, his beer slopping into the dust.

Helsby pushed him in the chest, and Moran fell to the ground. A couple of the fellas from the ranch helped him to his feet, and held on to him as he tried to pull away to get at the sheriff.

'Leave it, boss. He ain't worth it,' one of the hands said.

'Just get him sobered up, and out of town,' Helsby said to him.

He watched as the men hauled Moran over to the horse trough outside the saloon, and held his head under while he tried to kick his way free.

Helsby grinned as he went to the doc's office. The doc was an old man who had taken a bullet in the leg in the War Between The States. His skin was lined and leathery.

'Fred's in the back,' Doc Lennon said to him. 'A bullet in the back is what killed him.'

'He have any money on him?' Helsby asked, taking a cheroot from the doc and putting it between his thin lips.

Doc Lennon said, 'A couple of hundred dollars.'

Helsby lit the doc's cheroot, then his. 'Musta bin from his poker winnings.'

'I was in the saloon when he was playing,' the doc said, blowing out some smoke.

'See the Grissom kid in there?' Helsby asked him.

11

'The game was late Friday night. Today's Saturday.' Doc Lennon thought for a moment. 'He was in there.'

'Thanks a heap, Doc,' Helsby said. 'Notice anythin' else about Fred?'

'A whipping. Old marks. It'd be a long time back. Before he came to Red Rock. An' before you ask, there was nothing else.'

Helsby scratched his head. 'Thanks a heap Doc. I'll be seein' you.'

'Pleasure,' Doc Lennon said, waving his cheroot in Helsby's direction.

Helsby left the doc's office puffing on his cheroot. Fred Bennet still had money on him, so it didn't look like it was robbery. That whipping. From the expression on Doc Lennon's face it was a bad one, and it was an old one. Jake wondered if that had anything to do with the killing. Whatever it was, folks in Red Rock would still hanker after hanging the Grissom kid, because the way he figured it, once folks got an idea into their heads it took some getting out.

He took his time walking to the office, trying to work it out in his mind. Where would the Grissom kid go? The kid didn't have many friends. Something of a loner from what he could see.

Back in the office he hung his .45 on the peg, and flopped into the chair. The heat was sure getting to him. Helsby got up and took a scoop of

12

water. Water. He remembered something that Bill Thompson had said once. Bill Thompson, the memory came flooding back. Helsby suddenly felt cold at the memory of Bill Thompson.

'Shelby's Hole would be a good place to hide up fer a spell. Plenty of water, an' some good cover.'

He slammed the scoop on the floor, and jumped out of the chair. On his way to the door he remembered his rig.

'What's the hurry?' Jenny Thompson, Bill's daughter, asked him as he went out of the office.

Jake stopped dead and looked at her. The last thing he wanted to do was to talk to Jenny. He knew that she had feelings for him and under different circumstances he would have been glad to return them, but with what he carried it was out of the question.

'Jake,' she said calling him back. 'What is it? You've sure bin acting strange since Pa got shot.'

'Sorry, Jenny. Half the Circle B crew are out looking for Grissom. I want to be sure I get him before they do.'

Helsby hauled himself into the saddle, and galloped in the direction of Shelby's Hole. Shelby's Hole stood a couple of miles out of town. Helsby remembered that the town kids used to go swimming there. Nearby were a couple of deep caves set in the rocks, the kids would use them to play hide and seek in the summer or to stay out of the way if they were in trouble with their folks. It was the one place Grissom might go. Helsby just hoped that he might be there now.

Watching the hole, Helsby couldn't see any sign of Grissom. Using the tall grass as cover he moved towards the hole. For a while he listened. He couldn't hear anything. Looking across the water, he couldn't see any sign of Grissom at the caves. Maybe he wasn't there or maybe he had a rifle and was waiting for him.

Getting to his feet, Helsby moved forward as quietly as he could, skirting the edge of the hole. The dry grass snapped under his feet. He made it to the caves without collecting any lead.

He wiped the sweat off his face, and decided to call out. 'Dick Grissom, you in here?'

No answer. He called out again. Again no answer. Helsby put his gun away, and hunkered down. He had seen the leavings of a fire just inside the cave entrance. He ran his fingers through the ashes. The ashes were barely warm. He didn't think Grissom had left them.

Getting to his feet, he looked round and came across a set of hoofprints. He followed them with his eyes. They stretched off into the distance in the direction of Aurelia, a good-sized town a couple of days' ride away. Walking back to where he had left his horse, Helsby got mounted and rode back to Red Rock.

The door to his office was unlocked when he got there.

'Get him?' Matt Stone, the mayor of Red Rock asked him.

'Get who?' Helsby asked him, knowing exactly who he meant.

He didn't much like Matt Stone, mainly because he was quick to get his paws into anything that didn't concern him, like sheriffing.

'The Grissom kid,' he snapped.

Helsby didn't much like his quick temper either. He thought that if Stone carried a gun, he would have been dead some while back.

Helsby hung his hat and gun up, and then he took a scoop of water.

'No, I ain't got the Grissom kid yet. Bin out lookin' though.'

'You got a smart mouth on you, Helsby. It's gonna git you in trouble one of these days,' Stone went on.

'An' you'll be the first to know about it,' Helsby said.

'You got any ideas where Grissom is?' Stone asked in a more reasonable tone of voice.

'No, I ain't got any ideas where Grissom is,' Helsby snapped back at him.

'You'd better find him quick. Fred Bennet was gonna bring some big business to Red Rock,

15

includin' the railway, and we don't want folks thinking this is another Abilene or Dodge.'

'First I've heard about big business comin' to Red Rock,' Helsby said, his interest quickening.

'Yeah, Fred was gonna sign the papers in a couple of days. Some folks are comin' in from Aurelia on the stage,' Stone said.

'There's gonna be some disappointed folks on that stage. Still, maybe I can arrange it so we can fix up to have Grissom hanged instead. That'll keep them interested.'

'Helsby, you'd better start takin' this serious or we'll get somebody else to carry that star.' Stone's face was a mask of fury.

Helsby looked at him. 'If you can get anybody else right now, go ahead. I've had two run-ins with Les Moran from the Circle B. Fred was a popular fella, an' there'll be more trouble before long. An' I can't see anybody who's right in the head wanting to get snarled up in it.'

'Then get Grissom caught,' Stone said angrily. 'I'll give you a couple of days. An' if you ain't got him, Red Rock will have a new sheriff. Understand?'

'Yeah, I understand,' Helsby said wearily. 'An' suppose I catch him, an' we hang the wrong man, what then?'

Stone looked at him. 'Then we won't tell anybody. Grissom was a mean-mouthed kid, an'

16

he didn't like Fred, because he claimed Fred had run some of his beeves off.'

Helsby watched as the mayor walked out of the office.

TWO

He dug out another scoop of water, and drank it. Sitting in the chair, he thought about how much he knew about Dick Grissom. Two minutes later he realized it wasn't a whole lot. Grissom had run the ranch along with his ma since his old man died. He seemed to have spent most of his time on the ranch, the Rolling G or, as some folks called it, the Lazy G, which Helsby found appropriate considering how much work his grandpa hadn't done. He didn't even know if he had a sweetheart. Helsby conjured a picture of Dick Grissom in his mind. Not what you'd call handsome, but not the sort of fella who would scare the kids on Halloween. Maybe he did have a sweetheart.

Time to ask around.

Helsby walked to the general store on the next block. Everyday, you could find folks passing the time of day, and swapping gossip. Morgan, the fella who owned it, was serving a couple for Red Rock's biggest gossips.

'Hi, Sheriff,' Morgan greeted him breezily.

'Mornin' folks,' Helsby said, touching the brim of his hat.

'Any luck catching that awful Grissom boy?' Mrs Connaghty asked him.

'It's a terrible thing that happened, getting shot in the back like that. Sooner that young fella's under lock and key the better. You any nearer catchin' him?'

'No,' Helsby said. 'Talkin' of young Grissom, what was the name of that sweet young thing he was runnin' around with?'

The storeowner and the ladies hid their mouths behind their hands to conceal their smirks.

'I wouldn't call her no sweet young thing, not with her working the place she does,' Mrs Connaghty said, tossing the others a sarcastic smile.

Helsby started to feel uncomfortable. Maybe he'd asked the wrong people in the wrong place.

'Where does she work?'

Mrs Connaghty looked at him. 'She works over in the saloon. One of them soiled doves. Goes by the name of Lily Jeffords.'

'Thanks,' he said, touching the brim of his hat, and going outside.

*

'Where's Lily Jeffords?' he asked the barkeep.

The fella looked upstairs. 'She ain't workin' though. She's gettin' some sleep.'

'Do me a favour,' Helsby said. 'I need to talk to her now. Git yerself up there, an' tell her the sheriff wants to talk to her.'

'Anythin' you say, sheriff,' the barkeep said, putting his cloth on the pumps and going upstairs.

Helsby waited for him.

'She's gettin' some clothes on,' he said to the sheriff when he came down.

Helsby ordered himself a beer and waited. Eventually Lily Jeffords came to the bar. She was tall and attractive. Helsby guessed that she was in her early thirties.

'Drink?' he asked her.

'I've bin drinkin' rotgut whiskey all night, so if you don't mind, I'll pass on it.'

'I don't mind,' Helsby said.

'What is it? I didn't get much sleep last night, an' you comin' in so early hasn't helped things.'

Helsby looked round the bar. There were half a dozen fellas in there.

'Don't worry about them. They wouldn't know about what we're talkin' about. I guess it's Dick.'

'You guess right,' Helsby said, taking a drink.

'What do you intend doin' about him?' she asked.

'I gotta find him before I can do anythin' about him.'

'Not sure I get your drift,' she said.

'Guess what I'm tryin' to say is, it would be better if I find him first. Them Circle B boys are already lookin' fer a rope, an' a tree to toss it over.'

'I get yer drift,' she said. 'Look, supposin' I got him to turn himself in, and supposin' I knew where he was, what would you do?'

'Make sure he lived long enough to get a fair trial.'

'Yer crazy,' she told him, looking round the place. 'This town's already run out of folks with fair minds.'

'I know, but it's the best I can do.'

'You can get him up to Aurelia, that's what you can do,' the soiled dove told him. 'He'll get a fair trial up there.'

'Guess so,' the sheriff said. 'Pity I don't know where he is. Might save me some trouble if I did.'

'You come here agin tonight around ten, an' we'll see,' Lily said to him.

'Ten it is,' Helsby said to her.

'I might have a lead on where Grissom is,' he told Stone when he came out of the saloon.

Stone had seen him coming out of the saloon, and had gone over to meet him.

'Glad to see yer takin' this business seriously,' Stone said.

'Let's just hope somethin' comes of it,' he told the Mayor.

'Don't we both,' Stone said.

He watched Helsby go back to the office.

'Tell the boss I'm taking a few hours off,' Lily said to the barkeep.

'Got some private client lined up?' the barkeep said with a laugh.

'I should be so lucky,' Lily said.

She went to the livery, and mounted her horse.

Matt Stone watched her ride out of town. The barkeep had given him the word. Stone kept him and a couple of others on his payroll. She rode to the edge of the Grissom spread, then forked off the main trail, and hauled up outside a disused line cabin, and went inside.

'You can trust Jake Helsby,' she said to Dick Grissom, who was sitting on a crate in the corner.

'How do I know that?' he asked her.

'Because you ain't got no choice. You can run fer the border, an' even if you get across it you won't last five minutes over the line. You're so damn young. You just ain't got no choice. Helsby's a fair man, an' he'll do all he can for you.'

Dick Grissom wrestled with it for a couple of minutes, then stood up. 'I guess yer right. You gonna come in with me, Lily?'

'Sure, Dick. Just don't go tellin' nobody I helped you or they'll run me out of town, if they don't lynch me.'

Outside they got into their saddles. Stone drew his Winchester from his saddle boot and cocked it, and raised it to his shoulder. Why git my hands dirty, he thought. He lowered his Winchester and put it in the saddle boot. He followed them as far as the crossing to the Circle B land, then headed up to the ranch house. The crew of the ranch were in the bunkhouse. He knocked on the door.

'Les Moran here?' he asked Al Dawkins when the door was opened.

'I'll get him,' Al said, surprised to see the mayor.

Stone waited in the warm afternoon air for Moran to come to the door. Moran gave a surprised grunt when he recognized the mayor.

'You got a minute, Les?' the mayor asked him quietly.

'Sure.'

'An' close that door. It's about Grissom.'

'What about that little back shooter?' Moran asked, breathing rotgut fumes all over Stone's face.

'Got a hunch he's gonna be under lock an' key before morning. So if you want to get down there, an' give Justice a helpin' hand, now's yer chance,' Stone said, feeling pretty satisfied with himself.

If it all worked out, Grissom would be dead by morning. Lynched by a mob. That would give him the perfect excuse to get rid of Helsby, and his big mouth, and with Fred Bennet leaving no heir, and all the new business coming to Red Rock, he could end up a rich man.

'Thanks, Mayor,' Moran said eagerly.

'Call me Matt. Red Rock's gonna be needing a new sheriff before too long, and you seem to be the right man for the job,' Stone said.

'Yeah, thanks,' Moran said.

'OK, git yer boys over there.'

Stone left the ranch before Moran and the crew. When he got to Red Rock, he rode in by a back trail, and went into his house after he had put his horse in the stable. Inside, he poured himself a glass of redeye and waited for the shooting to start.

Helsby had gone round to the back of the saloon, and waited for Lily, and Dick Grissom. He didn't have to wait long. They rode down the alley at the rear of the saloon.

'You two OK?' he greeted them, his eyes straining in the dark to see if anybody had seen them. He wanted to get Grissom into the jail, and into a cell before they were caught in the open.

'Yeah, Jake, everythin's just fine,' Lily said softly as she looked up and down the alley.

'C'mon, Grissom, let's git over there,' Helsby said to the young fella.

'I didn't have nothin' to do with Fred Bennet gettin' shot,' he said, his voice a little shaky.

24

'Let's talk about it when we get to the jail.'

He followed Grissom out of the alley, and across the dark street. When he got to the office, he unlocked the door, and ushered Grissom inside.

'What were you arguin' with Fred Bennet about, the other afternoon?' he asked Dick, as he lit the desk lamp.

'Bennet kept lettin' his beeves stray on to our land, an' takin' off with some of ours along with his own. His spread has the biggest herd in these parts, an' we can't afford to lose any so I had it out with him. I could see I wasn't gettin' nowhere so I went back to our place.'

'Anybody see you?'

'Just a couple of the hands. I came into Red Rock to watch the poker. Fred was winnin', an' I came back to the ranch.'

'Anybody see you when you got back?'

Grissom thought about it. 'No, I don't think so.'

'I got to admit it's lookin' bad fer you. Nobody bein' able to say they saw you, an' you havin' high words with Fred.'

'Yeah, I can see how it looks, but I didn't shoot him,' Grissom said, with a real fear in his voice.

'Gonna have to lock you up, as much for your own protection as anythin' else,' Helsby said, taking the keys to the cells from the peg.

*

Outside, Les Moran was leading half a dozen ranch hands into the saloon. They headed straight for the bar.

'Set 'em up,' Moran yelled at the barkeep.

The barkeep looked at them, and guessed there was going to be trouble. He took a couple of bottles of redeye from the shelf, and half a dozen glasses.

'Here y'are boys,' he said.

Moran grabbed one of the bottles, and started filling up the glasses.

'C'mon folks,' he said to the whole saloon. 'Drinks are on the Circle B. To the memory of Fred Bennet.' There was a roar of approval as the crowd rushed the bar.

Lily was on the stairway. She watched for a moment, then decided to let Helsby know there was trouble on the way. Helsby had got Grissom locked up, and was going to make him and his prisoner some coffee when Lily came in.

'What's the matter?' he asked her.

'Moran's over in the saloon gettin' everybody liquored up. Figure they're gonna be comin' over here for Dick as soon as they've drunk enough courage.'

'You'd better get back over there, an' be careful nobody sees you.'

'Good luck,' she said to Helsby, and slipped out of the door.

As she hurried across the dusty street, she

heard the rising noise from the saloon. Once inside the saloon, she looked into the bar. It was almost empty.

Helsby took a shotgun from the rack, and broke it open. He pushed a couple of shells into the gun, and put a couple of spares in his vest.

Grissom was lying on the bunk, his hands beneath his head, staring at the ceiling. Helsby guessed that he might be thinking what the noose would feel like when they slipped the rough hemp over his head, and it started to nestle up against his skin. Then he would hear the final few words before they sprang the trap, and he took the drop.

'Coffee?' Helsby asked him, as he watched him lying on his bunk.

'I didn't kill Bennet, you've got to believe me,' he said.

'It ain't up to me,' Helsby told him. 'It's up to the jury. I just had to bring you in, which I've done.'

The kid said nothing else, but went and sat on his bunk, drinking his coffee. Helsby went back to the office, and sat at his desk, looking at the shotgun. Bill Thompson had a shotgun in his hands when Helsby went into the bank that night. There had been no sound, and the light Bill was using was on the floor shielded from the window by the door of the safe.

27

The stone coming through the window, and the drunken noise from the crowd dragged him back to Grissom. He looked at the clock. The hands had crawled up to twelve o'clock.

Midnight.

Helsby got up, took the shotgun, and went to the door. Moran was out in front of the mob, half-empty bottle of redeye in his hand, an angry, drunken expression on his face. Helsby felt the tremor of fear. He wanted to tell them they could have Grissom, and do what they liked with him, but he couldn't. He owed it to the Law, and to Grissom.

'You gonna turn Grissom over for what he did to Fred?' Moran shouted drunkenly, his stocky body swaying unsteadily on its short legs.

'Go to bed,' Helsby told the mob. 'I ain't givin' Grissom to you, an' if you try to come an' get him, a lot of you are gonna get hurt.'

A few of the mob looked towards their homes at the other end of town. One or two looked like they were going to go home, but Moran in his drunken state sensed the same thing. He took another swig from the bottle, and lurched round.

'Remember Fred Bennet. You've bin drinkin' his whiskey all night.'

'That's enough, Moran,' Helsby said, taking a step towards him.

Moran turned, and Helsby swung the butt of the gun onto his head. As Moran went down,

Helsby fired a shot into the air. The sound of the shot took the mob by surprise, and Helsby wondered how many of them would have risked it.

'OK, break it up,' he shouted.

The mob froze. Helsby fired the second barrel into the air. The mob wavered. Some looked at him, then started to drift away. That left the hands from the ranch stood in the middle of the street, and Moran lying at his feet. Helsby dropped the empty shotgun, and hauled out his .45.

'Get him over to the doc's,' Helsby said.

A couple of the hands picked Moran up, and carried him over to Doc Lennon's office.

'Everythin' all right?' Grissom shouted from his cell when he heard Helsby come back into the office.

'Sure, everythin's all right,' Helsby called to Grissom.

He opened the desk drawer and fished out the bottle of whiskey that he had inherited from Bill Thompson. He took one generous swallow, and put the whiskey bottle back in the drawer. Wiping off his face, he sat in the chair, wondering if Bill Thompson had ever been scared. He guessed not. Bill Thompson didn't know the word fear. Helsby wiped the sweat off his face again. This time it wasn't fear. It was the knowledge of what he had done to Jenny's pa. Helsby took the bottle

29

from the drawer again, and took another pull. Just as he got it in the drawer, Jenny walked in.

'I heard about what you did tonight. That's what Pa would have done. He'd have been proud of you,' she said, putting her arms round his neck. 'Real proud of you.'

Helsby wished he could get another drink.

Jenny pulled away from him. 'Not like you to take a drink while you're working.'

'Just needed a quick one.'

The answer seemed to satisfy her. 'Just as long as it's only one.'

'Yeah,' he said.

'I've got to get back. It's damn cold in these nightclothes and this shawl.'

Helsby walked her to the door, and watched her go down the street. The place was quiet by now. He looked across the street, and saw a shadow lurking in the alley. He jumped back into the office, and slammed the door, then drew the bolts across. He realized for a few minutes he had been silhouetted in the doorway. Looking out of the window, he could see nothing. Poking his head into the corridor, he could see that Grissom had managed to get to sleep.

THREE

For the rest of the night, he sat in his chair, his head occasionally falling forward into his hands. By the morning, he was bushed. Stone came in at eight. He looked pretty sour. Helsby had decided not to tell Stone that he was taking Grissom up to Aurelia, so he thought he would play for time by asking the mayor to get a deputy.

'After last night, I'm gonna need some help in here,' Helsby told him.

Stone looked at him. 'I ain't sure the town can run to a deputy.'

'Yer gonna have to do somethin',' Helsby said. 'Yer the mayor, so that makes it your responsibility.'

Stone snorted, 'An' yer the sheriff.'

'It's still your responsibility,' Helsby said, his anger beginning to rise.

Stone considered it. 'I guess yer right. I'll ask around, an' see what I can come up with.'

'Now's a good time,' Helsby said.

Stone took the hint, and headed for the door.

'Get some grub sent in fer me, an' Grissom.'

Stone went out of the office. Helsby made some coffee, and went through to Grissom with it.

'How are things out there this mornin'?' the kid asked him, taking the mug out of his hand.

'As far as I'm concerned they're nice an' quiet,' Helsby said.

'Thanks fer what you did last night,' the kid told him.

'Yer welcome,' Helsby said, as he turned to go back to the office.

Stoop, the fella who ran the café, came in with a tray covered by a cloth.

'Got some grub fer you, an' that low-down back shooter,' he said as he put the tray on Helsby's desk. 'Mayor's bin askin' round fer a deputy while yer on yer own, but I don't think he's been having much luck.'

'Guess not after last night. Half the town was out there with those Circle B boys.'

Stoop shrugged. 'I gotta be goin',' he said.

Helsby gave Grissom his food, and then went to eat his own. At eleven, Stoop came for the empties. He had nothing to say.

At twelve, Stone came in again. 'Sorry, Helsby, no takers. Yer on yer own 'til we can fix up a trial.'

'OK. Just keep tryin'.' Helsby left him to it.

Lily Jeffords came in. 'Got some bad news for you. You're on your own.'

'Stone came in an' told me,' Helsby said.

'Sounds like more bad news,' Lily said. 'There's talk goin' round about a crowd comin' over here again tonight, an' they mean it for sure.'

Helsby looked at her. 'I thought they'd had enough last night.'

'Somebody, I don't know who, has been stirring them up again,' she said.

'I can't stand a mob off agin. You got a spare horse fer Grissom?' he asked.

'Sure. He can use mine. Why?'

'I'm gonna git him up to Aurelia. Then find out who killed Fred Bennet, an' why.'

'So you don't figure Dick shot him?'

'I ain't sure. He'd bin arguin' with Fred. So what? Fred had a couple of hundred dollars on him. So why didn't the kid take it? That ranch needs some work doin' on it. I figure the kid would have taken it.'

'You could be right,' Lily said.

'Bring yer horse round back in about half an hour. It'll give me time to put the kid wise as to what's goin' on.'

'Yeah, but yer gonna have to be real careful. You can't trust anybody.'

Lily left the jail. Helsby went to the cells.

'C'mon,' the sheriff said to Grissom. 'We're gettin' out of here.'

33

Grissom hauled himself off the bunk. 'What's goin' on?'

Helsby told him.

'We'd better git a move on then,' the kid said.

'We've got a little time,' Helsby said. 'I've gotta tell you, make one wrong move, an' I'll put a bullet in you.'

'That's OK by me. I sure as hell didn't kill Bennet, but I'd sooner be shot than be lynched.'

Helsby took the irons from the drawer, and fixed Grissom up with them.

Lily Jeffords had gone back to the saloon and put some bread and beans along with a hunk of dried beef in a bag, and then went the back way along the alleys until she came to the livery stable.

She had almost made it when Stone caught sight of her. He followed her along the alley, curious as to where she was going and what she was up to. He watched her go into the stable.

Fender, the liveryman, was snoring in his little office, a half-empty bottle of redeye at his elbow. His grey wispy hair moved up and down as he breathed noisily out.

Lily saddled up Helsby's horse without wakening Fender, then she saw to the one she was going to lend Helsby to get Grissom up to Aurelia. She led them outside, with Stone watching what she did.

Helsby had got Grissom out at the rear, and was

34

waiting for her.

'Thanks, Lily,' Helsby said when he got Grissom into the saddle.

'Yer welcome,' Lily told him. 'Just get him up to Aurelia, an' sort this mess out.'

'Thanks a heap, Lily,' Grissom said. 'I sure won't fergit this in a hurry.'

'Just try and stay out of trouble. Yer just a bit wild,' Lily replied.

Helsby gigged his horse, and they rode quietly out of Red Rock.

Stone had seen Lily go back to the saloon. He figured she was up to something, but he hadn't figured out what. Then it hit him. He had just got a telegram from Aurelia about Judge Wallace. Saddling up his horse, he lit out for the Circle B. Moran was in the bunkhouse nursing a bottle of redeye and a sore head.

'Git some fellas you can trust. Helsby's taken Grissom out of jail. I figure he's taking him up to Aurelia.'

'Why's he goin' up there?' Moran asked, pulling on the redeye.

'Ol' Judge Wallace were sportin' with one of the soiled doves and his heart gave out on him. Damn near scared the soiled dove to death,' Stone said. 'Just make sure they don't get up to Aurelia.'

'OK,' Moran said.

He went outside to the stables with three of his

boys, and got mounted up, and headed after Helsby.

Helsby lead Grissom's horse through the night intending to put as much distance as he could between them and Red Rock. Daylight came, starting slowly by putting a pale wash across the sky, but then it started to go black again, with some heavy water-filled clouds coming out of the east. They rolled up quickly, racing across the sky, being driven by a wind that howled like a starving wolf. The wind scooped up the dust and threw it into the faces of the horses and the riders. Helsby tied his hat over his head with his bandanna. Then it started to rain.

He hauled his slicker out of the saddle-bag and put it on.

'You got one of them fer me?' Grissom shouted over to Helsby.

'Yeah, I got a spare in my saddle-bag, but I ain't in a position to get it on you.'

'You could trust me,' Grissom shouted, the wind dragging the words out of his mouth.

Helsby unfastened the irons and waited while Grissom put the slicker on. By the time he had got it on, the rain had started to fall, and the lightning had started to fork the sky. The two men rode hunched low against the wind and rain. It pounded against the slickers. The horses stumbled and staggered against the wind and rain.

Behind them, Moran and the boys from the

Circle B had run into the same thing.

'Hope we ain't gonna git two days of this,' Moran shouted above the wind.

Those behind him didn't hear him. They just kept their heads down, and hoped that it would soon stop.

Towards mid-morning it slackened off, and the clouds began to clear. Helsby hauled off the trail, and got out of the saddle. Like Grissom, the violence of the storm had taken it out of him, and the horses. He got Grissom off his horse, and took off the irons.

'Remember what I told you back there: make a run for it, and you'll get some lead between the shoulder blades.'

'Don't worry, Sheriff, I ain't that stupid.'

Helsby unshipped his gun, and broke it open. 'Never know when yer gonna need it,' he said, as he started to clean it.

They were off the trail, and were at the top of a low hill. After Helsby had cleaned the gun, he noticed the waterproof bag that Lily had tied to his saddle-bag.

'Somebody likes us,' he said, fishing the stuff out of the bag.

'Care for some?' Helsby asked, preparing to share it out.

Grissom smiled. 'Sure.'

The men ate in silence with Helsby watching the trail below them. Moran had not let the men rest, and had gone on when the storm passed. The storm washed out the tracks on the trail, and any sign that Helsby and Grissom had passed that way.

'We got some company,' Grissom said, as he finished eating.

Helsby, who had been seeing to the horses, came to his side. For a few seconds they watched the horsemen, and then Helsby grabbed Grissom's arm.

'Git back,' he said, pulling him away from the crest of the hill.

'Who are they?' Grissom asked, squinting against the sun that was pretty strong after the storm.

'Circle B. Reckon the short fella out in front is Les Moran. They're awful anxious to get a rope round yer neck.'

Below them, the Circle B boys kept going.

Half an hour passed before Helsby raised his head to look at the empty trail.

'We're safe now?' Grissom said hopefully.

'I don't think so,' Helsby said. 'Them fellas could figure out that they passed us, an' hole up until we caught up with them.'

'So what do we do?' Grissom asked. 'Go back to Red Rock?'

'Back into the rattler's hole,' Helsby said, looking at the trail.

'So what do we do?'

'Find another way round, an' hope we get to Aurelia before they figure that out. We'll go through Snake Pass, an' come out behind Aurelia, I'll deliver you to the sheriff there, an' go back to Red Rock, an' sort this mess out.'

He put the irons on Grissom, and got him into the saddle. They headed up in the direction of Snake Pass. Most of the time the land was flat and open. Both men kept watch for any signs that Moran had guessed what was happening, and might try to do something about it.

The riders pressed on during the day. The heat grew, and all the signs of the storm was wiped out. The earth became baked and cracked, and Jake felt the sweat running down his neck. A couple of times they halted, and took a drink from their canteens, and ate the food that Lily had fixed them up with.

Night came, and Helsby called a halt. They ate the last of the food before turning in.

'Should be there late tomorrow,' he told the kid, as night fell.

Moran was thinking the same thing, but he was a mite more worried. He had to get them before Helsby got the kid lodged in the Aurelia jail.

Helsby and Grissom spent the next day on the trail, and got to Aurelia just after nightfall. Aurelia was bigger than Red Rock. It boasted a sheriff and two full-time deputies, and a couple of part-time deputies who helped out at the end of the week when the miners came in to make free with their time and money.

Helsby hauled up outside the sheriff's office, and took the kid inside.

'Hi, Jake,' Cy Parker greeted Helsby when he came in with Grissom. 'It's good to see you. Got yerself a prisoner?'

'Not exactly,' Helsby told him. 'I wuz just wonderin' if you could put this young fella up for a while. I've got to be gettin' back to Red Rock in the mornin'.'

'Sure,' Cy said. 'Milt.' Milt was one of Cy's regular deputies. 'Lock this fella up.'

Cy waited until Grissom had been taken away, before indicating for Helsby to sit down. 'Now what's all this about?'

Helsby told him what had happened in Red Rock with Fred Bennet.

'An' you reckon he didn't do it?' Cy asked, as Milt returned to the office.

'No. I just don't see it somehow.'

'Any idea of who might have done it?' Cy asked him.

Helsby shrugged. 'I figured it might have something to do with his past.'

Milt came across with a mug of coffee. 'Talkin' about Fred Bennet, now it's goin' back aways, but there used to be a Bennet clan that lived twenty or thirty miles outta town. They had a younger brother, just up an' disappeared one day. The sheriff at the time, Sam Granger, went out to the spread an' found the family dead. All of them, except Fred an' his youngest sister. Can't think of her name right now. Never got to the bottom of it, but Sam reckoned that Fred did it. The girl never showed up either.'

'Sam Granger?' Helsby asked. 'He still alive?'

'Yeah, he lives with his wife a couple of miles out of town. I'm goin' to take these to them in the mornin'. Gonna take some pie, an' candy. Sam's still got a sweet tooth. Rita, my wife, fixed them. Sam ain't got too much money, an' he did a lot for this town. That OK with you, Cy?'

'Sure. Didn't figure you to have a charitable bone in that ornery body of yours,' Cy said with a laugh.

'Mind if I ride out and see him with you?' Helsby asked, taking a drink from the mug.

'Shucks, no,' Milt said. 'Be here about nine, an' we'll go out there. You got a place to stay for the night?'

'I've stayed here a couple of times. I'll check out the Golden Palace,' Helsby said. 'I'll be seein' you.'

When he went out of the office, he headed across town to the Golden Palace. It had been some time since Helsby had been in Aurelia, and he could see the place had grown a heap. There were a couple of new hotels, stores and the rail-

41

way had started to get in there. The Golden Palace was as it had always been, loud and garish. Its loud music and revelry could be heard down the street.

'Evening, Sheriff. Nice to see you,' the clerk behind the desk said.

'Evenin'. Got a room fer the night?' Helsby asked him.

'Sure have. Nice one at the rear,' the clerk said, turning the register.

'Thanks,' Helsby said, as the clerk came round to show him up to his room.

'Town seems pretty lively,' he said, as he followed the clerk up the stairs.

'It's the miners. They're in letting off steam. An' there's some folks from back East. They're bringing the railway to your neck of the woods.'

'So I heard', Helsby replied, recalling the conversation with Stone.

Helsby tipped the clerk, and lay on the bed. He was wondering what had happened to Moran. He'd make a point of finding out when he got back.

Suddenly, he didn't feel like sleeping. The idea seemed to have worn off him. He decided to go to the bar. Maybe he might meet the people the clerk was telling him about who were bringing the railway into Red Rock.

He saw them right off. Two men and two women

dressed like they were out for a night at a New York theatre. He guessed they must have had to take a heap of ribbing from the miners who worked the Snake River diggings.

'Beer,' he said to the barkeep when he got his attention.

'Comin' right up,' the fella said and pulled Helsby's drink.

Helsby took his drink, and went over to the group.

'Hi, folks,' he said.

'Can we do something for you, Sheriff?' The speaker was a beefy red-faced man with a heavy growth of side-whiskers.

'I'm Jake Helsby, sheriff of Red Rock.'

'Pleased to meet you, Sheriff. I'm Dan Harker. This is my wife, Beth. Samuel Davenport, my partner, and his wife, Sarah. We're going to be doing some business up your way before much longer,' Harker said, taking a drink from his glass.

'So I've bin hearin,' Helsby said.

Before he could go on, Harker beat him to it. 'We're going to buy the Circle B ranch from Fred Bennet.'

'I guess you don't know then,' Helsby said.

'Know what?' Dan Harker asked him.

'Fred Bennet's dead. Somebody shot him in the back last week.'

'That's terrible,' Beth Harker said.

The four of them exchanged glances.

43

'Sorry to be the bearer of bad news,' Helsby said. 'I guess this will change things,' he said thinking of the jobs that would have come up to Red Rock.

'Not at all,' Beth Harker said quickly. 'We'll get in touch with Mister Anderson as soon as the telegraph office opens first thing in the morning.'

Helsby took a closer look at her, and realized that she was a good few years younger than her husband.

'I'm sure we can fix something up with Mister Anderson,' Samuel Davenport said.

'I hope so,' Helsby said stifling a yawn. The heat in the Golden Palace was suddenly getting to him.

'You get much trouble up there with outlaws and rustlers?' Samuel Davenport asked Helsby.

'Not too much,' Helsby replied.

'When we last saw Fred Bennet he was saying that the sheriff, Bill Thompson, I think his name was, had been shot.'

'Yeah, Bill Thompson,' Helsby said, his mouth going dry.

'He said Thompson was shot by someone robbing the bank or trying to rob it, I don't remember which.'

'Trying to rob it,' Helsby said, his tongue getting thicker in his mouth.

'You know, Sheriff, you're starting to look very tired,' Beth Harker said, giving Helsby the kind of

44

look that he had seen a few soiled doves in a few saloons give him in the past.

'I've bin bringing a fella up from Red Rock so guess I'd better turn in. See you folks in Red Rock.'

FOUR

Up in his room, his sleep was shallow and restless, haunted by dreams of Bill Thompson, the money and the safe, and the shooting.

He got up early, feeling worse than the previous night. At the sheriff's office, he found Milt waiting for him.

'You look like how I felt after my twenty-first birthday party,' Milt said to him. 'Had any breakfast?'

'Grabbed a cup of coffee in the café. That was enough for me.'

'Not the best way to start the day,' Milt said.

They headed out to see the ex-sheriff of Aurelia.

Sam Granger was sitting in a rocking-chair that he had built for himself. He was smoking his pipe on his porch. He looked a fit, robust fella.

'Hi, Sam, it's me, Milt,' the deputy called out as he climbed out of the saddle.

When he got down, Helsby realized that Sam Granger must be almost blind.

'I've got some pie fer you,' Milt said. 'I've got a fella that wants to talk to you. He's the sheriff up in Red Rock, Jake Helsby.'

Granger held out his hand, and Helsby put his own into it.

'Howdy, Sheriff,' Granger said. His voice was deep and gruff. His moustache was brown stained with the tobacco.

'I was wonderin' if you could help me with a fella who used to live in these parts, a fella called Fred Bennet.'

Granger's eyebrows went up at the mention of Bennet's name. He put out his pipe, and knocked it against the porch rail.

'Fred Bennet?' he said, feeling his way along the rail.

'Fred Bennet. You know somethin' about him?' Helsby asked.

Milt had taken the stuff into Granger's wife.

'Sure,' Granger said. 'Killed his whole family, except Betsy, his little sister. Never found her body,' he said with an air of melancholy.

'The rest of the family?' Helsby asked the old man.

'Butchered them all in their sleep. Cut their throats. Place looked like a slaughterhouse when I got there.'

'How did you know something was wrong? Did

somebody tell you?' Helsby asked him.

'No, I was going to see Fred's old man. Fred was only seventeen. Came into town the day before. Back like a piece of meat. Bloodied and striped. I was going to arrest Charlie for it. Had a heavy hand. This time he'd gone too far. Charlie was a big one for the bible, an' Fred had taken up with some girl in town. Got to be honest, she wasn't quality folk. Some say she had a rep with the fellas, an' that's what musta got to Charlie. That's why he gave Fred the whippin' he gave him,' Granger said sourly.

Helsby leaned against the rail, and looked out over the empty land. Not another place for a good few miles. A man like Charlie Bennet could get away with almost anything. No help for the kid. Not a shoulder to cry on. One beating and one whipping too many, and Fred cracked. So why did he kill the rest of the family, and what did he do with Betsy?

'You seem like I felt when I found them,' Granger said suddenly.

'How's that?' Helsby said coming out of his reverie.

'Lost. You come across Fred Bennet?'

'He had the biggest spread round Red Rock,' Helsby said, hauling out the makings.

'Had? Something happen to him?' Granger asked.

'Somebody shot him in the back,' Helsby said,

putting a lucifer to the stogie.

'Bad way to end,' Granger said philosophically.

He felt his way back to the rocking-chair and sat down while Helsby smoked his stogie.

Milt came out of the cabin, and looked at them. 'You two finished yer business?' he asked them.

Helsby ground out the stogie, and nodded without speaking.

'We're finished fer now.' Granger said. 'If I think of anything that will help, I'll get Cy to wire you at Red Rock.'

'I'm obliged for your time,' Helsby said.

'Any time yer passin', the conversation would be welcome,' Granger said as he started to rock.

Helsby and Milt mounted up, and pointed their horses in the direction of Aurelia. Granger heard the misty figures ride away. Fred Bennet had been a good kid, a mite long-suffering. Fred had done more than his share on the ranch and that lazy brother of his, Frank, had done nothing to help. His ma had ignored it all, and let Charlie beat the hell out of Fred, but then maybe she had suffered to. Sam Granger sighed heavily, and started to rock steadily.

The two men rode along in silence, Milt thinking his own thoughts, Helsby thinking about what Sam Granger had told him.

'They treatin' you OK?' Helsby asked Grissom when he saw him in the cell after he and Milt got back.

49

'No complaints,' Grissom said, a mite nervously.

'Glad to hear it,' Helsby said. 'I'll let you know how things are goin'. Be seein' you.'

In the office, the deputy told him that Cy had gone for something to eat. 'Little Mex place across the street.'

'I saw it on the way in. I'll eat across there, an' say goodbye,' Helsby said as he went out.

He had started to feel hungry on the way back, and the thought of some hot food made him hungrier. As he started across the street, he heard a voice behind him.

'Good morning, Sheriff Helsby,' Beth Harker greeted him as he turned.

'Good morning, Mrs Harker,' Helsby said.

'Please. Call me Beth,' she said, closing the gap on them. 'You have no idea how sorry me and Dan were when you told us about poor Fred. We hope it won't be long before you catch whoever shot him.'

'It won't. Will you still be comin' to Red Rock?' he asked her as she came closer to him.

'I expect so. Dan and Samuel have great plans for Red Rock. Was Fred married? I know this sounds uncharitable to ask, but life must go on.'

'Fred wasn't married. Though he did have a sister, but she seems to have disappeared some time ago. Nobody knows what happened to her.'

Beth Harker pursed her lips and looked thoughtful. 'I'm not sure what will happen in that case. Do you know if he has any other family?'

Helsby thought hard. 'I'm afraid I can't help you there.'

Helsby backed away from her. She seemed to have been creeping up close to him. He didn't like the feeling of being hemmed in.

'Why, Sheriff, there's nothing to be afraid of,' she said, making up the ground between them.

'I'm sorry, Beth. I have to get back to Red Rock,' he temporized.

Beth Harker laughed. 'Are you shy, Sheriff?'

'No, Beth, just in a hurry,' he said.

'I'll let you go, then,' she said and turned to walk in the direction of her hotel.

Helsby hurried across the street to the café and went inside. Cy was sat facing the door. He waved his fork in Helsby's direction, then sank it into a piece of ham.

'Git what you wanted?' he asked Helsby as he signalled for the waiter to come over.

He ordered a fresh pot of coffee, and Helsby ordered breakfast.

'Got some background on Fred, but nothin' that's gonna help me, I think. Do you know what happened to Fred's sister?'

Cy shrugged. 'Wondered about that off and on over the years. Don't think Fred killed her. Nobody round here did.'

Helsby's breakfast came, and he started to eat.

*

51

Beth Harker had gone back to the hotel with the feeling that Sheriff Helsby hadn't exactly given her the brush off, but at least he wasn't interested. Being met with a lack of interest by any male was something she wasn't used to.

'You don't look in such a great mood,' her husband said when she walked in to the breakfast room at the hotel.

Beth feigned indifference. 'Did you know that Fred Bennet had a sister?'

Dan's mouth fell open. 'No, I didn't. It looks like things ain't gonna be plain sailing after all.'

'That's the bad news. The good news is that she's probably dead.' Beth Harker picked up a napkin, and shook it out, then pushed it into the top of her dress.

'Where'd you get this information?' Dan asked her, as he poured coffee into his cup.

'From that sheriff who brought Grissom in,' she said, holding the cup out for her husband to fill it up.

Dan Harker's eyes narrowed. 'You setting your cap at him now?'

'And if I am? You ain't exactly the man you were in that department, and don't you forget it.'

Dan Harker suppressed the boiling rage that had built up inside him when his wife told him about talking to Helsby. He knew from her tone of voice that she was baiting him. His hand clenched round the handle of the coffee-pot.

'You'll do it once too often.'

'I don't think so,' she said smugly. 'If you'd had any guts, you would have done something about it a while back. Now why don't you just eat your breakfast, and we'll figure out what to do about Fred Bennet's sister, if she's still alive.'

Dan didn't enjoy his breakfast.

Helsby collected some supplies for the trail, and headed in the direction of Red Rock. On the trail he gave some thought to Moran. He'd figured for a while that Moran was a troublemaker, and he needed to do something about him, but Moran hadn't done anything wrong, except getting drunk in public, and that wasn't a hanging offence. He couldn't prove anything right now. At the back of his mind, Helsby felt Moran would cause him more trouble.

He slept a night on the trail, under the star-filled sky. He made coffee, cooked some ham and opened a can of beans. In his saddle-bag he had put a half-bottle of whiskey. He opened it up and took a drink. Its warmth wound round his body like a woman's arms, and that made him think of Jenny and her father. One day soon, he figured, he would have to tell her.

Leaning against the saddle he put the bottle to his lips again, and took another drink. It's rawness warmed him again. For a third time he put it to his lips, and this time emptied it. Slowly, he fell asleep. The following morning, he cooked himself breakfast, saddled his horse and took to the trail for Red Rock again.

It was night when he got there. Helsby unlocked the office and went inside. It took him a few minutes to get the lamp lit. A few minutes later he heard the sound of shoes on the board-walk outside and Lily Jeffords came into the office.

'You get him there all right?' she asked Helsby.

'Eventually,' he said.

'That sounds like you almost didn't,' she said, taking a chair opposite him.

'Moran and some of the Circle B boys came after us, but we gave them the slip, and came in through Snake Pass.'

'But he's all right?'

'Sure, fixed up as snug as a bug in a rug in the Aurelia jail. Went out to see Sam Granger,' he said pulling out the makings, and fixing himself up a stogie.

'Who's Sam Granger?'

'Used to be sheriff over there when Fred Bennet lived there,' he said quietly.

'Fred Bennet lived there? Tell me all about it,' she said quickly.

Helsby did just that. 'Sam Granger reckoned Fred killed his family, except his sister, Betsy.'

'What happened to her?' Lily asked him.

'Nobody knows. Folks seem to think Fred took

54

her somewhere, but he didn't kill her.'

Helsby watched Lily's face; she seemed to be searching for something or trying to remember something.

'You OK?' he asked her.

'What? Yes. It's the hell of a story. Who would have thought that of Fred?'

'As you say,' Helsby replied. 'It's the hell of a story.'

'I gotta get back over there,' Lily said, getting up.

'I'll see you around,' Helsby said as she went out.

When she had gone, he fixed himself up some coffee and sat drinking it. It had been almost a week since Fred Bennet had been killed, and he was getting nowhere. There were no suspects. Nobody he could point the finger at, and he didn't think that Grissom had done it.

While he was sitting trying to figure it out, Stone and Moran were sitting in Stone's back room. Moran's failure to get Helsby and Grissom had left a sour taste in Stone's mouth, but he needed the fella opposite him.

'Don't loose no sleep over it, Les. You'll get another try at him, and this time you'll make it stick.'

'Sure will,' Moran said slurring his words.

Stone wasn't a bad fella, he told himself, pouring another measure into his glass.

'How are we gonna play it?' Moran asked.

Stone pretended to think for a minute. 'Dunno right off, Les. You get back to the Circle B an' I'll get word to you. Just finish up your drink and wait for my word.'

Moran swallowed the drink, then got up. The room was swaying a mite.

Stone guided him to the back door and gave him a hand getting up in the saddle. Stone watched as Moran guided his horse onto the back street. Going inside, he sat at the table again, and poured himself another drink. He cursed Moran for his stupidity. Helsby had got Grissom to Aurelia, and that meant he had no real reason for getting rid of Helsby, but he was going to get rid of him and his big mouth. He poured himself another drink, and decided to turn in. In the morning, he would go and see Fred Bennet's attorney, and maybe fix something up over the sale of the Circle B, after he had met the people who were going to buy it.

The stage rolled in at ten o'clock escorted by a cloud of thick trail-dust. The driver hauled on the leathers, and kicked the brake on. Dan Harker got out first, followed by Sam Davenport. They handed the females down while the shogtun tossed down the luggage. It hit the hard, dusty earth. Davenport took a step back, and hollered up to the shotgun.

'Be careful with our luggage. It ain't your cheap stuff. We bought that in New York, and it cost.'

'Sorry, fella,' the shotgun said, hiding a smirk. He didn't like monied folks the best of times.

Dan Harker ruffled himself up, but Stone stepped off the boardwalk to meet them.

'Be careful up there. Sorry about that, Mister Harker,' he smarmed.

Harker looked him over. Typical small-town politician, he told himself.

'That's all right, Matt,' Dan Harker said. 'I'm sure he didn't mean any offence by it.'

Stone had paid a couple of the local kids to carry the bags over to the hotel.

'We heard about Fred Bennet getting shot,' Dan Harker said when they got in the hotel. 'We've got to consider how this will affect things.'

'Don't you worry about that,' Stone told him. 'I'm going to see his attorney. I've a feeling Fred left a will. He was pretty hot on things like that. He didn't like loose ends, and that kind of thing.'

'We're pleased to hear that,' Beth Harker said, peeling off her gloves.

FIVE

Brett Anderson, Fred Bennet's attorney, had a new office with a blindfolded statue holding the Scales of Justice in one hand and a heavy-looking sword in the other. He hadn't been in too long, and when Stone walked in, he was just opening the mail the stage had brought in.

'Things picking up?' Stone asked him.

Anderson looked up from his mail with a sour look on his square face.

'Not so you'd notice,' he said. 'Thought things might have improved when Fred Bennet brought his business over here when his old attorney died.' He leaned back in the chair and looked Stone over, like he had a couple of times in the past.

'What can I do for you, Matt? You brought me any business over?'

'It was Fred I came to ask you about,' Stone began.

58

Anderson held up his hand. 'Could be stepping on unsafe ground here.'

'Probably am,' Stone said, deciding to take the bull by the horns. 'Did Fred leave a will? Only the folks who were going to buy that land, and the Circle B if it comes up for sale, came in on the stage.'

Anderson relaxed a mite. Now they were getting to it. 'Strictly speaking I ought to throw you out of here, and let Helsby know, but I think our interests are the same. We ought to be able to work something out whereby we all show a profit. I could sure use it. I've heard that you like to take your pleasures up in Aurelia, and they don't come cheap up there.' He held up a letter he had been reading. 'You're in a hole that's a thousand dollars deep.'

Stone gave him an angry look. 'What's that?'

'A letter from a little lady up in Aurelia. You owe her some money.'

Stone glowered at him. He could guess who the letter was from and what it contained. Anderson shrugged, folded the letter. Stone held his anger in check.

'Fred didn't leave a will. He's got no living family, so all we need is a will, and we're gonna need two signatures for that, and you're going to have to provide them. I've seen you talking to that little weasel Les Moran. I think you could use him, and find somebody else. Like I said, that's

going to be up to you. I'll look after this.'
Anderson tapped the letter and put it in the
drawer.

Stone wasn't too happy with this, but he could-
n't do much about it for now.

'I'll let you know how things are going,' Stone
said before he left the attorney's office.

He found Moran up at the ranch, helping break
in some horses. The place had started to look a
mite neglected, even after only a week without
Fred Bennet to keep his eyes on things. He saw
that the crew seemed to be losing interest in the
place.

Moran saw him, and dropped the rope he had
been holding. 'Didn't expect to see you out here,
Matt,' he said.

'I've come to put some money your way, if
you're interested.'

Moran's expression changed, and he started to
look interested.

'OK, I'm listening,' he said after making sure
that nobody else was within earshot.

'Sounds like it might work,' he said, when he
had heard Stone out.

'We're going to need another signature as well.
Maybe one of your friends over there would do it.
You'd both be well paid,' Stone said, eyeing the
hands who had stopped working, and were loung-
ing on the rail of the corral.

'I know just the fella,' Moran said after a few minutes.

'Can you trust him?' Stone asked.

'Sure I can,' Moran said. 'Mike Gilchrist. Nobody here knows it, especially the old man. He did time a while back. I don't think he'd want his pals to get to know about it.'

'I'll let you fix it up,' Stone said, reaching for the leathers of his horse.

'Who were those people I saw getting off the stage?' Jenny asked Helsby.

They were stood in his office, looking out across the street.

'Just some people who are gonna bring some business to Red Rock,' Helsby told her.

He looked at her. Her hair was copper coloured, and shone when the sun hit it. Her face was strong and not feminine; her eyes were as blue as the sky on a summer's day. Helsby pulled himself up. If he kept on thinking about it, he was never going to tell her about her pa.

She turned suddenly and caught him looking at her. 'Something the matter, Jake?'

The question caught him off guard.

'No, just thinking how beautiful you looked,' he said quickly.

'Jake, that's the first time you've ever said anything like that. You sickening for something?'

'No, hon, it's nothin',' he said quickly.

Jenny continued to look at him for a minute. 'Are you sure?'

'Yeah, I'm sure,' he replied more sharply than he had intended.

Jenny gave him an angry look. 'Just what is the matter? You've been like this since Pa got shot.'

'I'm real sorry, Jenny,' he replied trying to sooth her.

'I'm sorry too, Jake, I just don't believe you. Now tell me what it is. Is it something I've done?' The colour had risen in her face.

Helsby put his hands on her shoulders. 'Like I said, it's nothin'.'

She pulled away sharply, and gave him a hard look. He stepped forward intent on making the peace, but she moved quickly away just out of his reach.

'I'd better be goin'. I'll call in later to see if you know what the matter is,' she said angrily.

Helsby watched her go, an angry feeling building up in his chest. What the hell had Bill Thompson been up to trying to steal from the Red Rock Bank? He stomped up and down the office searching for an answer, but he couldn't find it. After a while he gave it up, and went outside. The first person he saw was Beth Harker coming along the veranda, a parasol held over her head to protect her from the sun.

'Makin' any progress on who killed Fred?' she asked him, her eye roving over Helsby's physique.

'Not yet. I was goin' over to the ranch to see if any of the hands knew anythin',' he told her, feeling uncomfortable at the way she was looking at him.

'I'd better not keep you then,' she said, twirling the parasol, airily.

'No, you'd better not,' he told her, edging away from her.

She turned and headed in the direction of Fred's attorney's office. Helsby watched her go for a minute, then climbed into the saddle, and guided his horse in the direction of the Circle B.

His investigation into Fred's death hadn't been progressing any. What made it harder was the fact that most people in Red Rock seemed to like Fred. The more he had thought about it on the way back from Aurelia, the more he was convinced that the answer lay somewhere in Fred's past. Maybe it had something to do with the whipping.

He rode into the yard of the ranch, and hauled on the leathers outside the cookhouse. At first he thought there was nobody around, then the door of the cookhouse up near the corral opened and he saw the ranch cook come out staggering under a heavy bucket of potatoes. When he saw Helsby, he dropped the bucket to the ground and wiped his face off with his apron.

'Hi, Jake,' he greeted the sheriff, the sweat starting to glisten on his fleshy face.

'Hi Mitch,' Helsby said, hauling out a Durham bag and offering it to the cook.

He took it eagerly. 'Yer a civilized man, Sheriff,' he said, a wide grin splitting his red face.

Both men were leaning on the rails of the corral. Mitch started to build himself a stogie. 'Guess it's Fred's killin' that brought you here.'

'You guess right,' Helsby told him. 'You know anythin' about Fred the rest of us don't?'

Mitch looked at him as he put a lucifer to the end of the stogie. Helsby started to build one for himself.

'Such as?' The blue smoke drifted from out of Mitch's mouth.

'Such as anythin',' Helsby said, watching the cook's face closely.

He watched as the man hesitated like he was wrestling with his conscience. 'OK, Mitch, what are you tryin' to tell me?'

'It's just that I don't mean no disrespect to Fred,' he said hesitantly.

'Relax,' Helsby said, putting the stogie between his lips, and lighting it. 'I won't go runnin' to the newspapers, an' tellin' them,' he said quickly, his restless grey eyes searching the yard.

'Fred had bin gettin' some letters from Trenton. A small place a couple of days up the trail.'

'Yeah, I know where Trenton is,' Helsby replied. 'An'?'

64

'An' he got worried by them.'

'How do you now they were from Trenton?'

'Saw them on his desk,' Mitch said nervously. 'I was takin' some grub to the house, an' they were lyin' on his desk, an' they caught my eye. Don't often get letters up here.'

'Don't suppose what was in them caught yer eye?'

Mitch looked offended at that. 'C'mon, Sheriff, what do you take me fer?'

Helsby said nothing, He had his own ideas.

'Well?' Mitch blustered.

'Get down off that high horse before you fall off it,' Helsby told him, taking a drag from his stogie, and pulling the smoke deep into his lungs.

'He just sorta changed after that. I've bin here longest, an' I know him better than these galoots here.' He swept his hand round the yard. 'Then after these letters came he seemed to be lookin' over his shoulder the whole time. Like he was expectin' somebody to come lookin' fer him. An' I guess they did.' Mitch took the remains of the stogie from between his lips, and crushed it under the heel of his scuffed boot.

'I guess they did,' Helsby said. 'Anyway, thanks, Mitch. If anythin' else comes to mind, let me know will you?'

'I'll do that,' Mitch said, picking up the bucket of potatoes, and going round to the side of the cookhouse.

As he got mounted, Helsby watched Mitch starting to peel the potatoes. Riding back to Red Rock, Helsby made up his mind that he would have to go to Trenton and find out who had written the letters and why.

SIX

Beth Harker returned to the hotel after speaking to Fred Bennet's attorney. In the hotel room she saw her husband and his partner and his wife sat waiting for her.

'Guess what?' she said to her husband.

He looked up at her. 'What is it?'

'Fred Bennet might have an heir. Someone who could mess up our plans for this place. Bennet's attorney hinted that he might be able to do something about it.'

Samuel Davenport lit an expensive cigar, and looked at her. 'Such as?'

'Such as,' Beth Harker said through narrowed eyes. She didn't need anything going wrong. She and her husband had spent a lot of money setting this deal up, and once they'd collected on it, it was Europe and the good life. 'Such as find a replacement for Betsy, that was the kid's name, and here's another thing. When he was about seventeen or so, he butchered his family, all except Betsy. Though why he stopped at Betsy, I don't know.' She added some emphasis on her words when she saw Sarah Davenport's face go green. Squeamish little bitch, she thought to herself.

The men looked at each other.

'Where's he going to find a replacement for her?' Sam Davenport asked.

'Don't worry yer head, Sam. That's the attorney's problem,' Dan Harker said, blowing out a banner of smoke, and sticking his thumbs in his suspenders. 'We're just going to have to go along with it.' He strolled across to the window, and looked down to the street. 'There ain't anything in this town we need worry about.'

Beth watched his back. He was an arrogant fool who might just get them hanged. 'I don't think that sheriff's any fool.'

Harker turned slowly from the window, the cigar hanging out of his fingers, the end glowing brightly. He raised it slowly, and said, 'I guess we all know what you think of Sheriff Helsby.'

Her face lit up with anger. Her high cheekbones flushed with fire, and her lips drew back in a venomous snarl. 'One of these days, Dan, you're gonna say the wrong thing to the wrong person and, if it's me, I'm going to kill you.'

Dan's face became white. The cigar almost dropped from his fingers. He struggled to say something, but just made the sound of a Thanksgiving Turkey who had just realized how near Thanksgiving was.

'Let's just all calm down,' Sam Davenport said, getting up quickly from his chair.

A little of the colour came back to Dan Harker's face, as he tapped the ash off the end of his cigar, and returned to looking out of the window. Sam Davenport and Sarah Davenport just looked at each other for a minute, then looked at Beth.

'Even if this Betsy kid turns up, so what? We'll just have to deal with her, an' I'm sure you know what I mean.'

The three other people in the room knew just what she meant.

'This is turning into something like a massacre,' Dan Harker said.

'You knew what we was getting into when we started this,' Beth Harker said with a quiet intensity that cut the air. 'It's OK fer you three: you've never bin poor. I have, an' I didn't like it. I ain't gonna be poor again.'

Samuel Davenport noticed, not for the first time, that Beth Harker had slipped into the gutter-level language of New York when she was angry. He would have liked to know her past, but she never spoke about it, and he, like Sarah, was too frightened to ask.

Beth watched them for a minute, saying nothing, then said, 'I'll get in touch with our friend in

New York, and get her here just in case we have to take care of anything.'

The three of them shrugged mentally. They were in too deep to say anything about another killing.

'Dan,' she said sharply. 'You've got the address. Get over to the telegraph office, and tell our friend to come down here. The usual fee – five thousand dollars, and expenses.'

Dan looked from under his bushy eyebrows. 'I'll go right away.'

'Sure you'll go right away,' Beth told him.

He got up from his chair, and scurried out of the room. Dan Harker went across the empty lobby, and out into the hot street. He turned in the direction of the telegraph office, still being unable to believe that his wife was going to order another killing. His face was pale, and puffy, and he cannoned into Jake Helsby just on the corner.

Straightaway, his soft fat body bounced off Helsby's lean, hard, muscular frame.

'You OK, Mister Harker?' Helsby asked him, steadying him in case he fell.

'Yes, fine,' Harker said, trying to regain his breath. 'I'm very sorry, Sheriff'

Helsby took a closer look at the fella. He seemed pretty nervous about something.

'No need to apologize,' Helsby said, watching Harker's face.

'I'm in a hurry,' Harker said. 'I've got an urgent telegram to get off.'

'I'll not keep you here jawin' then,' Helsby said, letting go of Harker's arm. Harker looked uncertain for a moment, then hurried off in the direction of the telegraph office.

Helsby stood watching him go. Later maybe he'd take a walk down to the office, and find out who Dan Harker was firing off a telegram to. He had a feeling that it wasn't going to be somebody good. Just a feeling.

Helsby started off again. He hadn't gone more than a few yards when he heard someone hurrying along behind him.

'Morning, Sheriff,' Matt Stone greeted him.

'Mayor,' Helsby said, affably.

'Anywhere near catchin' Fred's killer?' Stone asked him in a voice that said he knew Helsby wasn't.

Helsby watched the mayor's face, and knew exactly what he was thinking.

'Got a couple of leads.'

'Any of them go by the name of Dick Grissom?' Stone asked the sheriff.

'No,' Helsby told him. 'Got one up in Trenton, though. Thought I'd take a ride up there, an see if there's anythin' to it.'

'You'd be better off going into Aurelia and getting Grissom to confess to his wrongdoings.'

'Sure make things easier for you, Mayor. An' come to that. Have you got somethin' against Grissom that the rest of us don't know about?' Helsby asked the mayor, studying his face.

Stone bristled. 'What do you mean by that?'

Helsby shrugged. 'Nothin'. It's just that you seem in a hurry to get Grissom hung, an' that mob got started pretty early, considerin' I hadn't had Grissom in jail long enough to make him some coffee.'

Helsby knew that he was going fishing, but he wasn't too happy about some things. Like the fire near Shelby's Hole. He couldn't see Grissom needing a fire for any reason. Sure wasn't cold enough for him to need one. It was like somebody had been camping out up there. It was a plain fact that the weather had been unseasonably hot for a few weeks now. Maybe he'd take a ride over there, and see if he'd missed anything.

SEVEN

Helsby watched as several of the hands from the Circle B came into town. They looked tired and dusty and more than a mite saddle-weary. They dismounted outside the saloon, tethered their horses and went inside. Helsby wondered where Les Moran was. Crossing the street, he pushed his way through the batwing doors, and went inside. The hands were standing against the bar waiting for the barkeep to get to them.

'Where's Moran?' he asked the cowhands.

One of them was Mike Gilchrist. Helsby had never liked the look of him. 'Les is back at the ranch,' Gilchrist said truculently. 'Why are you askin'? Still got a beef with him?'

Helsby braced himself. 'I ain't got no beef with him. Thought maybe he had a beef with me.'

'A wisecrackin' sheriff,' Gilchrist said, brushing his black hair out of his face.

He was a big burly fella with dark eyes that

looked like they could flare up without much cause. Pushing his *amigos* away from the bar, he grabbed a bottle by the neck and smashed it against the top of the bar The glass showered outwards, and his *amigos* jumped back out of the way.

Gilchrist's eyes took on a shiny look as he came towards Helsby. Snatching his hat off, Helsby threw it at Gilchrist, who put up his hands to ward off the hat. Helsby jumped at him. He caught Gilchrist's wrist and twisted the glinting edge of the bottle away from his face. Gilchrist tried to drive his knee into Helsby's groin, but Helsby clamped his hand on Gilchrist's knee and held it hard. Both men tumbled into the sawdust.

Helsby let go of Gilchrist and got to his feet, before his attacker could come up for air. They circled each other warily, a grin on Gilchrist's face as he waved the broken bottle at the sheriff. Helsby moved in, and Gilchrist lunged at him, but instead of trying to catch Gilchrist's wrist, Helsby dived at his legs.

Gilchrist went down on top of Helsby, but the sheriff wriggled clear, and got to his feet. He stood over Gilchrist and brought the heel of his boot down on his wrist. Gilchrist screamed and let go of the bottle. From a face-down position, Helsby grabbed him by the scruff of his neck, and slammed him against the bar. The bar shook, and the glasses on it rattled. Pulling Gilchrist round so that he was facing him, Helsby hit him under the chin. The blow dumped Gilchrist on the other side of the bar.

He climbed slowly to his feet, holding on to the edge of the bar for support. The sheriff stood over him and took him by the shirt front and hauled him over to his side of the bar.

'I ain't got a beef with Moran,' Helsby said between his teeth. 'But I sure got one with you now.'

Gilchrist looked at Helsby with his eyes half open, a dreamy look in them. Pulling the cowhand's gun from the holster, and sticking it in his belt, he pushed him towards the door of the saloon.

Outside, townsfolk watched as Helsby pushed him into the jailhouse.

'How did you know I have a beef with him?' he said, when he had Gilchrist in a cell.

The cowhand had come round. He felt his chin as he sat on the bunk.

'After what you did outside the saloon, it's obvious you've got some kinda beef with him. So quit stallin', Sheriff.'

'Moran had it comin'. Nearly got an innocent man lynched. There was that trouble on the way to Aurelia, so you quit stallin'.' Helsby was perched on the edge of the wooden table inside the cell.

'How'd you know Grissom is innocent?'

Gilchrist asked.

'It's no more my business than yours,' Helsby said to him. 'A fella's entitled to a fair trial.'

Gilchrist scowled. 'The hell he is.'

'Have it your way,' Helsby said, going to the door. 'I'm goin' up to Shelby's Hole. I'll be back in a couple of hours. I'll let you out then, if I remember.'

The trail was wide and easy to follow until he got out of town and got closer to Shelby's Hole. Then it started to peter out until there was only a narrow track, almost covered with brown sundried grass.

Helsby walked across to the entrance of the cave where he had found the remains of the fire. The ashes were cold now, but the hoof prints and the boot prints still looked pretty fresh. There had been no wind or rain to obliterate them. Helsby stuck a stalk of grass in his mouth.

At the entrance to the cave he could still follow the hoof prints in the direction of Aurelia. Strange, he thought, as he chewed on the grass stalk. Why would anyone camp here when there was a town not too far away? He went and took another look at the boot marks. Whoever it had been, it was no kid hiding from its folks or spending a summer's day swimming in the hole. This was an adult. Somebody full-grown.

Back at the cave's entrance, he looked the way

he had come, and off to the left. In the direction of the Lazy G land off to the east was the Circle B land, and the trail which Fred Bennet would have to ride down to get back to the ranch after a night in Red Rock playing poker.

Mounting up, he rode in the direction of the Circle B. He stopped when he could see the ranch house, and the trail leading into the yard. Dismounting, he looked at the grass.

'He musta bin a tall fella,' he mused to himself, pacing out the flattened grass where he figured the assassin had lain waiting for Fred Bennet.

A few feet away from where the assassin had lain, Helsby found a single shell case lying in the grass. He picked it up, and rolled it between his fingers. The bright sun caught it as he rolled it.

Helsby put it in his vest pocket, and had another look round. The boot prints were, he figured, the same as those up at the hole. He took another look at the ranch house below. It was the same as last time, starting to look neglected like everybody was losing interest.

He rode to Red Rock, and took the shell case to the gunsmith. Frank Smith had been a gunsmith all his life, and had settled in Red Rock a good few years ago.

He was in the back of the shop when Helsby got there.

The gunsmith wore glasses, perched on the end of his beaky nose. That and his sandy hair made him look more like a schoolteacher than the deadly shot that he had been in the War Between the States.

He looked over the top of his spectacles when Helsby walked in.

'What can I do for you, Sheriff?' he asked, taking off his spectacles and putting them on his work bench.

'I'd like you to take a look at this,' Helsby told him.

Frank took the case off Helsby and looked at it.

'What do you make of it? Is it one of yours?' Helsby asked him.

'Where'd you get it?' the gunsmith asked him.

Helsby scratched the side of his face. 'Out near the Circle B.'

'Fred Bennet's place?'

'Yeah, Fred Bennet's place. What can you tell me about it?' Helsby liked Frank, but Frank liked to gab. Helsby put it down to him not being married, and not having much in the way of company.

'Not one of mine. Seen it's like before though,' Frank said slowly, admiring the case.

'Don't stop now,' Helsby said, trying to keep the irritation out of his voice.

'This came from the gun that put an end to Fred's life?'

'The same,' Helsby said, gripping the edge of the counter.

'It's a work of art. Handmade. Marksman's bullet. Saw them in the late unpleasantness we had with the gentlemen from the South. Marksmen would fashion their own. Didn't trust nobody else.'

'Anybody from these parts could have made it?' Helsby asked him.

'I could have, but I didn't,' Frank said. 'No, nobody from round here would have the tools that I know of,' Frank finished.

'If you're looking for its owner, you're looking for a professional with a gun. A hired killer, an' they ain't that common hereabouts.'

'Thanks a heap, Frank,' Helsby said, taking the case from the gunsmith's hand and putting it back in his vest pocket.

'Yer welcome,' the gunsmith said, taking his spectacles from the bench, and putting them on.

Helsby strolled out of the gunsmith's feeling a mite happier.

'What are you lookin' so pleased about?' Stone asked him when he got into the office.

Helsby's good feelings dropped a notch when he saw Stone.

'Got a suspect in the Fred Bennet killin',' he said, taking a seat behind his desk.

Stone gave him a sharp look. 'Who is he?'

Helsby shrugged. 'I don't know yet.'

'That mouth of yours, Helsby,' Stone snapped at him.

The sheriff shrugged. 'I've a feelin' he's gonna be back here before long.'

'You going to let me in on this little secret of yours?' Stone asked him, keeping his temper under control.

'Sorry mayor, if it's all right by you. I'll keep my own counsel for now.'

The mayor looked at him. 'I think it's your duty to keep me informed. I am the mayor of this town.'

'If I keep you informed, somebody else might get informed. Like Les Moran, and his pals from the Circle B.'

'What are you accusing me off?' Stone demanded, leaning over the desk.

'I ain't accusin' you of anythin',' Helsby replied. 'Just sayin' it's the hell of a coincidence them fellas turnin' up on the Aurelia trail just when me an' Grissom were out that way.'

It was Stone's turn to look surprised, but then maybe Stone had just worked it out for himself.

'Haven't you got somethin' else to do?' Helsby said. 'I've got a prisoner to turn loose.'

Stone went out of the door, his face red with anger. He'd fix Helsby, he promised himself again.

Gilchrist was sitting on the edge of his bunk, smoking a stogie, when Helsby went through to him. His head came up sharply when he heard the sheriff.

'Time to go,' Helsby said, putting the key in the lock, and turning it.

'About time,' Gilchrist said, grinding out his stogie on the cell floor.

'Who told you I was takin' Grissam up to Aurelia?' he asked Gilchrist suddenly, as he came out of the cell.

Gilchrist stopped, and was about to say something, then stopped himself and grinned at Helsby.

'Yer a sharp one, Sheriff,' he said, going up the corridor.

'The drop's even sharper,' Helsby replied.

Gilchrist's face suddenly turned white. 'What d'you mean by that?'

'Fred Bennet's bin killed, an' I figure there's gonna be more, an' if I'm any judge you'll be in it somewhere.'

'Wanna watch yer mouth, Sheriff. You might find yerself gettin' a piece of lead.'

'Git through the door,' Helsby said.

Gilchrist gave a snarl, and went out into the street.

EIGHT

When he had gone, Helsby walked down to the telegraph office. Ronnie Webster was just closing up for the day. Ronnie was seventeen, and lived with his mother at the end of town in a small house. Mrs Webster had been a widow for a few years, and had got a red-hot brand of religion since her Scottish husband had gone to his rest on the Heavenly Highlands. She ruled Ronnie with a rod of iron.

Ronnie gave Helsby a worried look when he saw him come through the door.

'Wuz just closin' up fer the day,' he said, taking off his eyeshade.

'I can see that, Ronnie. Won't keep you long.'

Ronnie became suspicious and worried. He had some magazines in the back from New Orleans that if his ma saw them she would consign him to hell along with the magazines.

'Don't look so worried,' Helsby said with an

easy grin. 'Just need some information from you.'

Ronnie looked at him feeling a little relieved. 'Sure, Sheriff. Anythin' you need.'

'Fella come in earlier today, this mornin', I think it was. Dan Harker. Just need to know who he sent a wire to.'

Ronnie Webster felt his mouth dry up. 'Can't do that, Sheriff. Against policy. Confidential.'

Helsby gave Webster a man of the world look. 'We're both grown-up fellas,' he said, and watched Ronnic preen himself. 'We can all keep secrets.'

Ronnie watched the sheriff's face. 'What do you mean?'

'I mean I won't tell anybody about you giving me the name and address of the fella that telegram went off to, an' won't go givin' away your little secret to yer ma.'

Helsby figured most young fellas had a secret. He had.

Ronnie licked his lips, and visualized his ma reading out his list of sins in the new meeting house. He felt the hot fires of hell burning his ass for all time.

Helsby watched him. 'You just leave the pad with the name and address on the counter and go in the back. Nobody will know if I've seen it or not.'

Ronnie gave the sheriff a dubious look. He brought out the pad.

'I'm going to the back for a couple of minutes,' he said, and pushed the pad towards Helsby. Helsby waited for him to go then turned the pad round.

The name and address meant nothing to him. He wrote them down on a spare sheet of paper. Ronnie came back a couple of minutes later.

'Thanks,' Helsby said. 'This stays strictly between you an' me.'

Outside, he wondered what Ronnie Webster's little secret was.

It was getting towards night now, so he headed up to Stoop's for some grub. The place was almost empty when he got there but he felt the hostility of the customers towards him. All the conversation died as he went up to the counter.

Stoop came from behind the curtain. 'What'll it be, Sheriff?' he asked Helsby.

'Don't mind, so long as there's plenty of it, an' it's hot,' Helsby said. 'I'm going to sit at the back.'

'Right,' Stoop said.

Helsby went and sat down. While he was waiting, he noticed some of the customers' heads turning his way. He knew they were talking about him.

Morgan, who had gone in for something to eat just after he had closed the store up for the night, came over to him.

'You gonna bring Grissom here for his trial?' he asked Helsby.

'We ain't got a judge. Old Judge Wallace departed for someplace happier,' Helsby told him.

'We can wait,' Morgan went on.

'Bet you can,' Helsby replied, watching his food go cold. 'Trouble is I want him tried fair, not by a rabble, an' I don't want him lynched by a rabble led by a no-good punk like Les Moran.' He picked up his fork, hoping that Morgan would take the hint, but Morgan didn't.

'This is the best place to try Grissom. Everybody in town knows that no-good little troublemaker,' he said, thrusting his face within inches of Helsby's.

'That's the trouble,' Helsby said, cutting up a piece of meat, and edging it on to the prongs of his fork. 'Everybody knows him, an' it ain't like everybody's got an unbiased point of view.'

'This ain't gettin' us nowhere,' Morgan said.

'It sure ain't gettin' my hunger put to bed,' Helsby said, putting the fork into his mouth.

Stoop came back with his coffee, and put it on the table. Morgan went back to where he was eating, and the talk started up again.

Helsby ate steadily, taking the occasional drink from his coffee. While he was eating he wondered how Grissom was getting on in the Aurelia jail. From there he went to thinking about his ma, and how she was getting on without him.

NINE

As he was clearing his plate, Lily Jeffords walked by Stoop's café on the other side of the street. He watched her go down in the direction of the Lucky Lady. Grissom's only friend as far as he could see. He took the piece of bread and mopped the gravy up with it. As he put it in his mouth, he remembered the bag of food that she had tied to his pommel.

He stopped chewing. Lily Jeffords and Dick Grissom, an unusual pairing, he thought. Whatever their relationship was it wasn't soiled dove and client. It was as if she was taking a motherly interest in Grissom – or sisterly. Grissom had no sisters but Fred Bennet had Betsy. Mopping the last of the gravy with the last of the bread, he put it out of his mind, pushed the chair away, and left the payment on the table. At the door he saw Lily Jeffords going into the saloon.

It was a quiet night, and there was no trouble in

any of the saloons. Just after midnight the town was all closed up. Helsby took a couple of drinks from the bottle of redeye in the drawer and turned in.

Early the next morning, he went to the general store.

'Just want some stuff to get me up to Trenton. Beans, jerky, an' some hard biscuit,' he told the store owner.

Morgan filled out a gunnysack for him, and sat it on the counter.

'What are you goin' up to Trenton fer? Something to do with Grissom?'

'Could have,' Helsby told him, picking up the sack, and putting the bills down. Helsby went out to the hitch rail, and fastened the bag over the saddle horn.

'Goin' some place?' a voice said behind him.

Lily Jeffords had come across from the saloon. She was still wearing her dressing-gown, and looked like she'd been up all night.

'Goin' up to Trenton to check on a couple of things,' Helsby told her, holding on to the leathers of his horse.

'Good luck,' she said, holding her hand to her eyes to shade them from the morning sun.

He touched his horses flanks and followed the trail out of town and up to Trenton.

It took him two days to get there. The nights had

started to get cold. Helsby built up the fire, laid his Winchester next to his saddle blanket, and got out the half-bottle of redeye, and took a good swallow before settling for the night. His sleep was fitful as he dreamt of the sound of Bill Thompson stumbling against the safe door as Helsby came into the bank from the rear entrance.

'What's goin' on Bill?' Helsby asked, as a cat and dog started to curse and spit at each other.

Bill had looked at him with a look of surprise on his face. 'Thought you were goin' over to see Jenny,' he said.

'I was,' Helsby had said. 'But I figured somethin' was wrong, so I came over here.'

Thompson licked his lips. 'Ain't what it seems.' A wad of bills in his hand, a sack in his other.

'What is it, Bill?'

Thompson coughed, a dry hacking cough. 'I need the money.'

'Yer crazy, Bill,' Helsby said. 'Just put the money away, an' we can talk about gettin' you out of this mess.'

The sweat on Bill's forehead shone, and the glow from the lamp gave him a ghostly look. Helsby noticed for the first time how drawn and gaunt his features had become.

'What's the matter?' he asked, taking a firmer grip on his .45 as it started to feel pretty heavy in his hand.

'I just need the money,' Thompson went on.

88

'You in some sorta trouble?' Helsby asked him.

'Jake, for God's sake,' Thompson went on. 'Let it go, for God's sake. I just need the money.'

'I can't let you do it,' Helsby said. 'It's the sort of thing we're here to stop. What's the matter with you?'

'Jake, just let me take the money.' Thompson was pleading by now.

'Can't let you do it,' Helsby said.

'You've got to,' Thompson pleaded.

'No, Bill, I don't. I'm goin' to stop you,' Helsby said, watching Thompson's face.

Thompson was starting to look wild-eyed.

'You gonna shoot me, 'cos that's what it'll take,' he said, his voice rising.

Helsby watched as the bundle of notes in Thompson's hand started to shake.

He felt his gun hand shaking.

Suppose it came to shooting Bill Thompson, could he do it?

'Put the money in the safe, Bill, an' we can go outside, before anybody else comes in here.'

'Jake, you ain't listenin' to me.' His voice was almost strident.

'Calm down, Bill, or somebody will hear you, an' if they do come in here there's gonna be nothin' I can do fer you.'

The cat and the dog had quietened a mite.

Bill screwed up his eyes. 'Jake, you got to give me a break.'

As Helsby was about to answer, the cat and dog started up again. The dog gave out a fearsome yell, and Helsby's finger tightened round the trigger. The gun went off throwing a hunk of lead into Bill Thompson's chest. Thompson was slammed against the open safe, the bundle of notes falling out of his hand, and scattering as the paper band broke.

Helsby saw him slide to the floor, his heart almost stopping and his mouth going dry. He looked round the darkened room. The only light was from the lamp on the floor. Outside, the cat and the dog were still swapping blows. Helsby bent down. Bill Thompson was dead. He saw that straight off.

The quarrelling pair outside had settled their differences, and had gone their separate ways. Helsby cocked his head and listened. He couldn't hear the sound of running feet, so he guessed that no one had heard the shot. Quickly, he gathered up the bills, and put them in the bag that lay at Bill's feet.

Once he got outside, he looked up and down the street. It was empty, the saloons had closed down an hour back. Dropping the bag on the floor, he walked to the entrance of the alley, and fired three shots into the air, and waited.

It took a few minutes, then people started to show up.

'What's been going on?' Matt Stone asked him.

'Sheriff's bin shot,' Helsby said. 'Some fellas were tryin' to rob the bank.'

'Where is Bill?' Stone asked him.

Helsby jerked his head in the direction of the bank.

'He dead?'

Helsby nodded.

'You're the one that's got to tell Jenny. If yer up to it. You don't look so good.'

'I'm OK,' Helsby lied.

'You'd better go an' do it,' Stone said.

Helsby made his way through the crowd. As he got to Thompson's house, the front door opened, and Jenny came out on to the veranda. Helsby took a step back and woke up. He was sweating heavily, and his bandanna was stuck to his neck.

TEN

Grabbing the pommel of his saddle, he hauled himself up. The fire had died down and the ashes fell in on themselves sending up a shower of sparks. Helsby reached under the saddle, and found the bottle of redeye.

The first long swallow burned its way down the back of his throat. Wiping his lips, he put the bottle under the saddle again, and sat looking up at the sky. Dawn was not far off. He lay down again, and tried to sleep, but it wouldn't come. When the sun was riding the horizon, Helsby got up, and took another pull from the bottle. It went down wrong and he started to cough. A harsh raking cough like Bill Thompson had in those final few days. Helsby spat into the ground then built up the fire again. He cooked breakfast, then ate it slowly.

It was round noon when he got to Trenton. An old prospector pointed him in the direction of the sheriff's office.

'Fred Bennet, you say?' The sheriff of Trenton sat behind his desk, a thoughtful look on his skinny face. 'Not a name I know and I know most folks in these parts.'

Jim Walker had been the sheriff for a couple of years, and Helsby had told him why he was in Trenton.

'You got one of them letters on you? Might be able to recognize the handwriting.'

Helsby took the letter, and passed it to the sheriff.

Walker read it carefully, and slowly, which made Helsby guess that his reading wasn't all that great. He watched Walker's eyes go up and down the script a couple of times, until he finally shook his head.

'Can't say I recognize it. Thought it might be Mister Beaufort's at first.'

'Who's he?' Helsby asked.

'Runs the new school in town,' Walker said. 'I guess it might be a good idea to take a walk down there, and see if he recognizes it. Reckon them kids will be having their midday meal about now,' he said, looking at the gold watch he had in his vest.

The school was a new building, just outside town. It had been painted white, a picket fence ran round it. As they got closer, Helsby could hear the noise of children playing noisily outside.

Walker pushed through the gate, and went up the tidy path to the schoolhouse.

William Beaufort was sat at his desk at the far end of the room, eating his lunch. He glanced up from his newspaper when the door creaked.

'Good morning, Sheriff,' he said with a grin, as they came down the centre aisle.

'Mornin', William,' the sheriff said. 'This is Jake Helsby. He does my job in Red Rock.'

Beaufort wiped his hands and mouth on a bright red napkin and stood up, his hand held out in Helsby's direction.

'This is business, I suppose,' he said.

' 'Fraid so,' Walker said. 'Care to show him the letter, Jake?'

'Wonder if you recognize the handwritin'?' Helsby said, passing over the letter.

Beaufort took it, and ran his eyes over it. 'Child's handwriting,' he said after a few seconds thought.

'Got any idea which kid?' Helsby asked him.

Beaufort leafed through the pile of exercise books on his desk, and pulled the bottom one out.

'Sylvester Slater,' he said thoughtfully. 'Good scholar, but his handwriting needs some work. Take a look.'

Helsby ran his eye over the work. Yes, it was the same handwriting.

'Sylvester in any kind of trouble?' Beaufort asked.

Helsby shook his head. 'No, he ain't in any trouble. I'd sure appreciate it if you didn't say anythin' to him, though,' Helsby said.

'No, I won't,' Beaufort said. 'You sure the lad isn't in any trouble?'

'Dead sure,' Helsby assured him. 'An' thanks fer yer help.'

They walked out of the school. At the bottom of the steps Walker put his hand on Helsby's arm and pointed to a young fella who was talking to a couple of girls.

'That's the Slater kid,' he said.

Helsby watched him for a minute. 'His folks live near town?'

'A couple of miles out. Why? You want to go an' see them?'

'If his old man wrote this letter, I sure want to see him. What sorta place they got?'

'Small farm. More of a smallholdin',' Walker said. 'Came here a few years back.'

Walker got his horse from the livery, and they saddled up.

The Slater place was three miles out of town, surrounded by good farming land. They came to the house after riding through a darkened wood with low overhanging trees.

'That's the place,' Walker said, pointing to a small cabin in a shallow valley.

'What sorta fella is this Slater?' Helsby asked, tipping back his hat, and wiping the sweat off his face with the back of his hand.

'Mean kinda fella,' he said.

Helsby took out the makings, and passed them to Walker.

'Can't figure how a woman like Esther Braddock got married to a bad fella like him.'

'She come from decent respectable folks?' Helsby asked, flicking ash off the end of his stogie. 'They got any more kids besides the little boy?'

'Dunno, heard talk of them havin' a little girl before they came here.'

'Where'd they come from?' Helsby asked Walker.

Walker thought for a while. 'Place called Aurelia.'

Helsby gave him a sharp look. 'Aurelia?'

'Yeah, you know of it?'

'Yeah. We'd best be gettin' down to the Slater place.'

They gigged their horses down the slope. There were no gates leading up to the house, just a well tended vegetable patch on either side of the trail.

'Esther's work. She keeps it goin',' Walker said.

As they climbed down, the door opened, and Esther came out to greet them.

'Good mornin', Sheriff. What brings you out here?'

'Sheriff Helsby from Red Rock wants to speak to your husband about this letter. He around?'

'He's out back fixin' up the fence. Want me to get him?'

'If it ain't a heap of trouble,' Walker said.

Both men waited while Esther disappeared round the back of the cabin. A couple of minutes later they both came back. Frank Slater was a small fella with sly foxy features, and quick moving eyes that never seemed to catch you full in the face.

'Let's go on inside,' Walker said.

Esther led them into the cabin. In spite of the bright sunlight outside, it was dark inside the cabin.

'What's this all about, Sheriff?' Frank Slater demanded.

Walker pulled out the letter and thrust it under Slater's beak of a nose.

'It's about this letter that you got yer boy to write to Fred Bennet,' Walker said, taking the letter out of the creased envelope.

'What about it?' Slater demanded. 'It's just a letter.'

'We can see it's just a letter,' Helsby snapped at him.

'So I wrote a letter to Fred Bennet,' he said.

Walker scowled at him.

Slater looked scared.

Helsby grabbed him by the shirt front.

'No, you got yer boy to write a letter to Fred Bennet, an' that's pretty low.'

Slater was wriggling against Helsby's grip.

'Tell me about the little girl,' Helsby said, tightening his grip.

'Did Fred Bennet put you on to me?' Slater said, almost choking.

His face was turning purple. Helsby eased off a mite.

'Fred Bennet's dead. Somebody put a piece of lead in his back late last week.'

Slater suddenly turned white.

'It wasn't me,' he gulped. 'I was here all last week, an' the week before. Ask Esther.' He tried to turn his head sideways, hoping that Esther would vouch for him.

'He was here,' she said reluctantly.

Helsby eased the pressure a mite more, and Slater started to breathe a mite easier.

'Now,' Helsby said. 'The little girl, Betsy. Tell me about her.'

'Fred Bennet left her at our place near Aurelia. He gave Ma fifty dollars: all the money he had in the world. Bin savin' up to run away since he was twelve. Saved every dime he ever got so he could get clear of that place.'

'OK, Slater, just tell us the rest,' Walker said, impatiently.

'Ma kept her. Raised her like she was one of us. Saw she had some schoolin', went to church. Like I said, raised her like she was one of us.'

'Then?' Helsby said.

'Then one night she just ran away. I always figured she would. Betsy kept herself to herself. Like she was frightened of somethin'.'

'How come you got to find out where Fred Bennet got to?' Helsby asked him.

'I was doin' a bit of work for the ranch just up the trail. Driving some beeves up that way. Saw this fella arm wrestlin' with another fella, out on the trail. I thought it was Fred. Then they both took their shirts off to cool down in the creek, an' I saw the marks,' Slater shuddered. 'I can still see them now. You see, when Fred dropped Betsy off he was in a bad way, an' Ma bathed him, an' put somethin' on to ease the burnin'.' Slater shuddered again.

Helsby let go of him. Slater slumped to the floor, and lay gasping for air until Esther came to pick him up.

'He's just weak,' she said.

Helsby and Walker said nothing. Helsby looked at Slater, who was leaning against the wall.

'You got a likeness of Betsy or somethin' to show what she was like when she was little?' Helsby asked him.

Slater thought for a minute. 'When Betsy an' us were little, a fella came by the cabin lookin' fer somethin' to eat. Ma gave him some bread, an' dried beef, an' the fella said he'd paint all of us. Ma said that was all right, but she wanted somethin' special for Betsy on account of how Ma figured she needed to be made to feel she was somethin' special.'

'I'd like to see it if you've still got it,' Helsby said.

'Last time I saw it, it was in that ol' trunk in the corner,' Slater said. 'Just you fellas wait, an' I'll find it.'

He scuttled across the room, and opened the rusty trunk.

'I try to keep him off the bottle,' Esther said. 'But there's some fresh made lemonade, you're more than welcome to a mug.'

'Sure wouldn't say no to that,' Walker said, his voice thick with the trail dust.

'Me too,' Helsby said.

Esther filled the mugs while the stuff from the trunk mounted round Slater's legs. Esther handed the two men the lemonade.

'Thanks a heap,' Helsby said, taking a mouthful.

The lemonade was ice cold, and cut through his thirst like a knife. Helsby drained it, and put the mug on the table.

'Some more?' Esther Slater asked him, picking up the jug.

Helsby was about to accept the offer, when Slater came over with the miniature. Holding it out, he showed it to Helsby and Walker. Both looked at it.

'Recognize her?' Walker asked Helsby.

Helsby took it out of Slater's grubby hand.

'Yeah, I think so,' he replied. 'I'd like to borrow this. I'll get it back to you,' he said to Slater.

Slater's face had a doubtful look on it. Helsby reached into his vest pocket, and took out two dollars, and put them in Esther's hand.

'OK. Just be sure I get it back,' he said to Helsby.

'Promise,' Helsby said.

'What did you git outta that?' Walker asked Helsby when he got outside.

'Got an inkling as to who's behind the shootin',' Helsby said. 'Not someone you'd know.'

'You goin' back to Red Rock now?' Walker asked him.

'There's a couple of people I've got to talk to,' Helsby said when they got back to Trenton. 'Thanks fer yer help, an' thank the school teacher as well.'

'I'll do that,' Walker said. 'An' let me know how it pans out.'

Helsby stayed long enough to fill up on his supplies, and buy another bottle of redeye. It was late afternoon when he headed up to the main trail that would get him to Red Rock.

ELEVEN

Brett Anderson was in the cathouse in Aurelia. He was sitting on the bed in the back room. The woman opposite had auburn hair and was passably good-looking. Her hair flowed down past her shoulders, and the languid movements of her arms as she brushed it made it sweep down like a river shining in the winter.

She glanced up to look at Anderson's reflection in the mirror.

'Thanks for getting me that money off Stone, but it still only entitles you to one freebie.'

Anderson got up from the bed and straightened out his clothes. He crossed the room until he was standing behind Mary Dillon. He took hold of her hair and stroked it. Mary pulled away abruptly.

'Quit it. I said one freebie, an' that's all.'

Anderson laughed and moved to the dressing table.

'Stone says you did some acting before you fell on hard times and had to change your profession.'

'So what if I did?' She was beginning to get angry as she was reminded of her promising career cut short, and how she had to become a soiled dove to make a living.

'How would you like to do some more acting?' Anderson asked her.

Mary snorted, disdainfully. 'Where am I gonna git an acting job? You see the fleapit they built here?'

'No, yer gonna be playin' somebody that's probably dead, an' there's gonna be ten thousand dollars. One big pay off. After it's all over you're going to have to get yourself down to Mexico or someplace were they won't recognize you.'

Mary Dillon stopped brushing her hair. 'I'm listening,' she said.

It didn't take long for Anderson to outline the plan he and Stone had figured out.

'Ten thousand dollars,' she mused when he had told her. 'OK, I'm in. You sure this Betsy Bennet is dead?'

Anderson looked at her. 'We ain't certain, but if she does show up, me and my associates will take care of her.'

Mary looked at him. 'They'll hang us for that.'

'If they catch us. For ten thousand it's worth the risk,' he said, as she started to brush her hair again.

103

That afternoon, Anderson headed back to Red Rock. He camped out on the trail, and got in late the next day.

Stone was waiting in his home when he got there.

'How'd it go?' he asked the attorney, handing him a glass of redeye.

Anderson took it, and sat in the chair opposite the empty fireplace.

'It went pretty well,' he said taking a drink. 'Only thing that bothers me is that Mary was a mite nervous about what would happen to us if this went wrong. I don't think she cottons to the fact that she might make a farewell appearance on the scaffold.'

'We won't have to worry about that. Dan's wife had got some plans for her,' Stone said coldly when he had sat down.

'What a blood-thirsty bitch she is,' Anderson said casually.

'That's part of the reason she called on her friend again,' Stone told him. 'An' you got that will fixed up yet?'

Anderson grinned contentedly. 'Sure have. You got them fellas to sign it?'

'Moran's got a buddy of his to sign it,' Stone said with an air of satisfaction.

They drank a toast to themselves, and Anderson went back to the rooming-house where he was staying until he got himself a place of his own.

Dan Harker was sitting in his hotel room seething angrily. Beth was out again. The third night in succession that she had been out. She had been out for most of the day as well. The second night they had been in Red Rock she had come in pretty late, her face flushed, and her hair riding free of the band she usually wore to keep it tidy. He knew right off where she had been. They had high words, but she was unrepentant.

'If you can't supply me with what I want, I'll go somewhere I can, and find someone who will provide me with it.'

He sat in the chair, smoking an expensive cigar, blue clouds hovering round his head. He heard the sound of footsteps outside on the landing. The key rattled in the door and it swung open. Beth was surprised to see him sitting there smoking.

'I thought you would have been in bed. I told you I'd be late.' Her voice was waspish and challenging, baiting him to start another argument.

'And just who is it you're seeing now?' Harker got up from the chair.

For a moment, he held on to the sides of it, staggering against the table that held the bottle of redeye.

'Starting' to hit that stuff pretty regular these days, aren't you?' she said, taking off her gloves and dropping them on the table near the window. 'You in the mood for another row?' she asked him.

'You got to be careful,' he said, with a slur in his voice. 'Folks ain't stupid round here. They see you playing fast and loose with anything in pants, they're gonna ask themselves what we're really doing here.'

'Let them ask. Just a bunch of backwoods hicks, as far as I'm concerned,' she said, her voice filled with contempt. 'The devil take them.' For the first time in a long time the faint trace of Irish came out of her mouth.

Dan Harker watched her, the effects of the redeye getting the better of him. Lurching towards his wife, he made a lunge for her throat, his hands out in front of him. Beth stepped aside, and pushed him. Dan Harker felt an expression of anger and rage going over his florid face.

Standing over him with an expression of contempt on her face, she said, 'You look even more stupid than you usually do. I'm going to bed, you make yourself comfortable in that chair.'

Once she had slammed the door behind her, she started to get undressed, hanging her stuff up in the closet. She would have to do something about Dan, she decided. He was becoming a liability with his drinking. Once they'd got this deal out of the way, she would do something about him. At five thousand dollars it would be cheap at the price. She might be able to get the others out of the way, and get their share as well. She got between the sheets feeling better than she had done since she had left Mike Gilchrist a couple of hours back. As usual she slept soundly.

The next morning, a boy came to the hotel.

'What do you want?' the desk clerk asked him.

'Wire for Dan Harker,' the sassy kid replied, holding out the wire.

'An' it's Mister Harker to you,' the desk clerk said, snatching the wire out of the kid's hand.

The kid looked up at him. 'Don't I get no tip?'

'I'll ask Mister Harker for one for you. Now beat it, before I toss you out.'

The kid ran for the door, looked back at the clerk, and pulled his tongue out at him. The clerk shook his fist and the kid disappeared out of the door.

Half an hour later, Dan Harker came to break-fast, and the clerk handed him the wire.

'Thanks,' Dan Harker said, giving the clerk a tip, and going into the breakfast room.

He was still pretty het up with Beth after last night. When Beth came in, he put the wire in front of her without a word. He said nothing while she opened it and read it.

'From our friend?' he asked her.

It was a rule that the killer's name was never mentioned. The killer was always referred to as 'our friend'. When she was informed there was another commission for her in Aurelia, the telegram had been addressed to a warehouse in New York.

'Our friend will be in Aurelia in a couple of days,' Beth Harker said when she had finished reading it. 'I'll be out again tonight.'

Dan Harker said nothing. He knew where she was going.

Mike Gilchrist was waiting at the edge of town, his horse hidden behind the gunsmith's shop. When he saw Beth coming his way, he stepped into the middle of the street, and signalled to her. She altered her course and came to him. He caught her round the waist and guided her round to the back of the gun shop.

'How are you feelin', honey?' Mike Gilchrist said.

'Just fine,' Beth replied, as her mouth sought his.

Gilchrist held her tight against him. They kissed long, and hard, before they pulled away from each other.

'I sure hope you've got some more of that,' Beth said, breathlessly.

'As much as you can handle,' Gilchrist said with a grin. 'But not here, an' not right now.'

Gilchrist got himself into the saddle, and pulled her up beside him. They galloped towards the Circle B land. A couple of minutes after they had ridden out, the door of the privy opened and the gunsmith came out. Under the moonlight, he watched the line of dust disappear among the low foothills.

TWELVE

Ronnie Webster came into Helsby's office early the next morning.

'Got a copy of that reply for you,' he said, taking a piece of paper from his trouser pocket.

Helsby took it from him, and opened it. 'Thanks, Ronnie,' he said, tossing the kid a coin.

Ronnie lingered for a couple of seconds.

'I expect you've got things to do, an' you don't want to leave old man Fletcher alone in there,' he said.

'No, I guess I don't,' Ronnie said. He had been hoping to pick up something in the sheriff's office to impress his friends with.

Helsby waited until he had gone before he read the message.

Stone came in a couple of minutes later. 'You got anythin' to tell me about Fred Bennet's murder? You been up to Aurelia to get Grissom to own up to what he did?'

110

'Speakin' of Aurelia, I'm goin' up there in a couple of days,' Helsby said truthfully.

'In a couple of days? What's wrong with tomorrow or today?' Stone snapped at Helsby.

'It ain't convenient,' Helsby said, holding his temper in check.

Stone fumed at him. 'We're going to be getting a new sheriff before long,' he said calming down a mite.

'We've had this before,' Helsby said, standing up.

'I figure we're gonna be having it again,' Stone told him.

'If you're the mayor, why don't you go an' do some mayoring or somethin,' Helsby told him.

'An' that might just be finding a way of getting rid of you,' Stone said threateningly.

Helsby took a copy of the telegram that Ronnie Webster had given him from his drawer and read it again. Ronnie's handwriting was only just legible.

'I'll be coming into Aurelia on the 5th of this month.'

It had the name S. Smith on it.

That would give him time to get up there, and with Cy's help, put a face to the name. He thought about wiring Cy and telling him that he was on his way up, but that would mean that Ronnie Webster would know what was in the telegram, and he might just tell his pals, and the

Harkers might get to know about it. In the end he built himself a stogie, and sat at his desk smoking it. Stubbing out the stogie in his mug he went down to Morgan's store, and got himself fixed up with stuff for the trail. He was about to get a half-bottle of redeye, then thought maybe it was turning into a habit. Helsby gave it a miss, and put the stuff into a gunnybag, tied it over his saddle, and took to the trail.

The night was cold, and he wrapped his hands round his mug of coffee for the warmth. Helsby slept. Bill Thompson didn't come into his dreams, but when he woke he still felt that he had to tell Jenny, and soon, before it got too hard. It was the same the next night. He would have to tell Jenny.

Cy was glad to see him. 'Business?' he asked, with a grin.

'Business,' Helsby said, getting into a chair. 'There's a fella comin' in on the stage tomorrow.'

'Got a name?' Cy asked him, settling in the chair opposite.

'Just S. Smith,' Helsby told him.

'Want him arrestin'?' Cy asked him.

Helsby shook his head. 'Nothin' to arrest S. Smith for,' he said.

Cy looked across the desk at him. 'Anythin' to do with Fred Bennet?'

'Could be. I went up to Trenton a couple of

112

days ago. Thought I had it all sewn up.'

'Then somethin' else came along?' Cy said with a rueful smile.

'Somethin' else came along,' Helsby said. 'Anyway, I'm goin' across to the hotel, an' get myself fixed up with a room. Stage still come in at twelve?'

'Twelve on the nose,' Cy replied.

'I'll get back here about half past eleven, just in case he's early,' Helsby said, pushing himself to his feet. 'I'll follow him. See where he takes me.'

He registered at the hotel.

'Same room as last time, Sheriff?' the clerk asked him.

'That'd be just fine,' Helsby said, dropping his saddle-bag to the floor and taking the pen off the clerk.

The clerk turned round, and took the key from the board and handed it to Helsby. When the clerk had gone, Helsby put the bag on the bed, and opened it up. Taking out a clean shirt, he washed his face and put the shirt on.

Sam Granger was rocking on the porch, smoking his old pipe, when Helsby got there.

'Was in the area, so I thought I'd call in to see how you were,' Helsby said after he had hitched his horse to the rail.

Granger felt his way along the veranda rail.

'How's it goin' with Fred Bennet?' he asked Helsby.

Helsby came up the rail and followed Granger along to his rocking-chair. Helsby sat down beside the ex-sheriff.

'Think I'm makin' some progress with it, but at the same time I ain't sure.'

'You sound like a man that thinks he knows his own mind,' Granger said with a grin, tapping down the hot tobacco in his pipe.

Helsby built himself a stogie, and pulled out the lucifers. The light flared quickly, and he put it to the business end of the stogie.

'Want some coffee?' Granger's wife had come out from the house without them hearing her.

She was tall with a slender figure, and a head of silver hair. Helsby guessed in her younger days she would have turned a lot of heads.

'Thanks.' He hesitated, looking for her name.

'Mary,' she said with a smile. 'Bet you could manage a slice of cake that Milt brought in.'

Helsby laughed. 'Sure could.'

Mary disappeared into the house.

'How near are you to findin' Fred's killer?' Granger asked, sucking on the pipe.

'Got a likeness of Betsy when she was a kid. Got it off the folks Fred left her with.'

He went and got it out of his saddle-bag, then stopped. There would be no use showing it to Granger.

Behind him he heard Granger laugh. 'I fergit

114

sometimes,' Granger said.

Mary came out holding a tray with some mugs, and small plates. She put them on the table next to her husband.

'Jake was sayin' that he's got likeness of Betsy,' he said to his wife.

'Wonder what she looks like now,' she asked quietly.

Helsby handed it over. 'I think I know who it is,' he said, 'but I can't see her shootin' Fred Bennet.'

'You didn't know her all her life, and people change a heap,' Mary said, handing Helsby a slice of the cake, and putting a mug into her husband's hand.

They chewed the fat for a spell, and then Helsby headed back to Aurelia.

'How is the old fella?' Cy asked him when he got back.

'Fine, an' smokin' like a chimney,' Helsby laughed. 'Anyways, I'm gonna get over to the saloon, an' get a couple of drinks an' something' decent to eat. My own trail grub's just turning my stomach.'

'See you in the mornin', about half past eleven,' Cy said, watching Helsby go for the door.

Helsby had a peaceful night without any dreams of Bill Thompson. It was just on half past eleven when he got across to Cy's office.

115

'Guess the best thing to do would be to take a walk to the stage office, and get Martindale, the manager, to point this fella out to us when he gets in.'

Helsby agreed with him.

Henry Martindale was a fat pompous man with an air of his own importance.

'This is what we want you to do,' Cy told him in the back office. 'When the stage gets in there'll be a fella on it by the name of S. Smith. We just want you to point him out when he comes in here to turn in his ticket stub. Got that?'

'I've got that, Sheriff. I'd have to be stupid not to,' he said haughtily.

Cy gave Helsby a sideways look.

'Sheriff Helsby an' me will be waitin' in here,' Cy went on. 'Better get our stars off.'

They went and sat in the corner, in a couple of rickety chairs, and started to read out-of-date newspapers. They didn't have long to wait until Helsby heard the stagecoach rattling down the street. There was a snort from the team, and the slither of the coach as it stopped outside the stage office.

Helsby looked at Cy. Both looked at Martindale. Martindale looked pale and nervous.

Outside, the doors of the stage opened and shut. A bag was tossed from the roof and hit the dry earth with a thud. The driver and the shotgun climbed down. The boardwalk creaked as somebody came to the door. The door opened.

Helsby gave Martindale a quick look, then looked back at the paper.

'Just came to hand in my ticket stub.' The fella was tall, and dressed in city clothes. He handed the ticket stub over to Martindale, who was struggling not to look at the men reading the papers.

Helsby tossed him a glance as he turned the page of the paper. Martindale looked at Cy, and shook his head.

Helsby got up as casually as he could and walked to the door. The fella who had handed his stub to Martindale came to the door. Helsby moved to one side, and he went outside.

Helsby watched him go down the street, and into the hotel.

'Anybody else on the stage?' Helsby asked the driver, who was getting ready to take the horses round to the back where he could water them.

'No,' he said. 'Only the woman, but she got us to let her out at the edge of town. Said somebody was waitin' fer her.'

'Cy, git out there an' ask this fella what the woman looked like. I'm goin' to the edge of town an' see if I can see anythin'.'

It shook Helsby. All the time he had assumed that the assassin would be a man. It had never crossed his mind that he might be hunting for a woman.

He left Cy with the driver and ran down the

boardwalk. At the end of the street he looked round, but couldn't see anybody.

Helsby got his horse, and rode to the edge of town, but there was no sign of the woman.

THIRTEEN

While Helsby was heading for Red Rock, Mary Dillon was coming in on the stage. Anderson had gone to Aurelia again to see her. He couldn't give her much in the way of background as far as Betsy Bennet was concerned but he didn't reckon it mattered. Nobody knew her, and he had all the paperwork as far as the Circle B went, now he had Moran and Gilchrist's signatures on a will he had forged.

Mary Dillon was still a bit worried about the whole thing, but Anderson had fixed her up with a $500 advance in cash, and that helped ease her nerves a mite.

Anderson met her as the stage rolled into Red Rock.

'You're lookin' as pretty as ever,' he said as he escorted her to his office. 'We'll get you fixed up in a hotel as soon as you've met our other partners.'

They walked along to Anderson's office with Mary Dillon holding onto his arm.

'Good morning, Lily,' Anderson said, raising his hat as they strolled passed Lily Jeffords.

The soiled dove, still suffering from a hard night, and hard liquor, barely acknowledged them as they passed.

'You keep low company these days, Anderson,' Mary Dillon said softly. 'How come you know her?'

'She's been in Red Rock for a spell. Some fella took a knife to her, an' I had to defend him in front of Judge Wallace.'

Mary Dillon's interest picked up.'Did you get him off?'

'No, Judge Wallace wasn't in a very good mood; the jury was in a worse mood and he got five years in the State prison.'

'Must remember to forget about you if I get in any kinda trouble,' Mary Dillon said, as they came to Anderson's office.

Mary Dillon felt like a prize heifer when they came to look her over. Right off she knew what Dan Harker was thinking, and she didn't like it. When it came to his wife, she could see that they had something in common. Both of them had shared the same profession at some time. She discounted the other two.

Beth Harker stood up to meet her, with the same recognition in her eyes.

'Pleased to meet you, Betsy,' she said, taking

hold of her hand.

'Same here,' Mary Dillon replied.

Dan Harker squeezed her hand, and his eyes lingered over her body. Stone was sitting in the corner watching them.

'OK, folks,' Anderson said. 'We all know why we're here. As far as we're all concerned, this is Betsy Bennet, from now on.'

The others nodded.

Helsby got in that night. He opened up the office, and lit a lamp. The place was warm, and stuffy. He opened a window and let in the night breeze. Opening up the drawer, he took out the bottle of redeye and took a drink. Straightaway he regretted it. The night was too warm, like the night he had seen Bill Thompson.

The sweat broke out on his forehead, and a couple of minutes later he shuddered as Bill Thompson's ghost crossed the office. Helsby shook his head.

At the end of the block he could see the light was still on in Stoop's place.

He crossed over and went in. There was only him and Stoop in there.

'How's it goin'?' Stoop asked him.

'How's what goin'?' Helsby replied.

'I guess you know what I mean,' Stoop said, giving him a hard look.

Helsby wiped his mouth with his hand. 'Just

serve me some chow,' he said angrily.

Stoop went through the curtain to get the stuff. Behind him, Helsby heard the door open and close.

'Hi, Jake,' Lily Jeffords said to him, as she came to stand by him at the counter.

'Hi yerself,' Helsby said to her.

The soiled dove looked at him. 'You don't sound in the greatest of moods.' She spoke quietly, and Helsby looked at her again. 'Not gettin' anywhere with Grissom?'

For a moment Helsby paused. 'Might be onto somethin'. Came across it in Trenton.'

'Trenton?' Lily asked him, her voice quick, and interested. 'Gonna tell me what it is?'

'Sorry, Lily, gotta see how it pans out first of all,' he said, as Stoop came in with his grub.

'What can I do for you, Lily?' he asked her.

'Just somethin' on some bread, an' some coffee. Things are slow tonight.'

'Things are slow here,' Stoop said, indicating the empty chairs. 'Had some folks in earlier. Come up from Aurelia. Reckon they're gonna bring the railroad through.'

'Met them up in Aurelia,' Helsby said, watching Lily Jeffords' face.

She glanced at him.

'They were anxious to know whether Fred Bennet had left a will on account of him bein' dead.'

'What did you tell them?' she asked him casually.

'I didn't know anythin' about a will. Just that he wasn't married, an' had no heir. Did have a sister at sometime, but nobody ever seen neither hide nor hair of her. Folks I've spoken to reckon she's dead.'

A faint flicker of emotion came over Lily Jeffords' face but it came and went in a second. Stoop came in with the coffee and a couple of ham sandwiches. He put them in front of the woman. She drank the coffee quickly like she was real thirsty. She moved the sandwiches around the plate just taking a couple of bites.

'Gotta be goin' back to it,' she said suddenly, and, dropping payment on the counter, went outside.

Stoop picked up one of the sandwiches, and looked at it. 'Can't see a heap wrong with it,' he said, taking a bite out of the piece of bread Lily Jeffords had left. Helsby said nothing. He was busy thinking about the look on Lily Jeffords' face. Stoop finished the sandwiches Lily Jeffords had left.

Finishing up his grub, and drinking the coffee, Helsby left the café and went back to the office. For a while he waited, expecting Jenny to show, but she didn't. When it was getting on towards midnight, he took a shotgun from the rack, and pushed a couple of shells into it, and a couple more into his vest pocket. He wasn't expecting any trouble, but Moran might decide to take a shot at him.

He stepped out onto the porch. The street was empty, except for a couple of horses hitched outside the saloon. He recognized one of them as Les Moran's. Helsby was tempted to go across and see what he was up to, but it might look like he was victimizing him. He carried on along the board-walk with only the sound of crickets coming from the patch of dead ground at the edge of town.

At the edge of town he crossed the street and started back on the opposite side. Reaching the saloon he saw that Moran's horse was still there. It nickered as he passed. The noise from the saloon wasn't too bad, so Helsby kept on walking.

Reaching the far end of the street, he was about to cross and come back along a back street when a hunk of lead passed his head. Helsby threw himself into the dust and rolled over, hoping to catch sight of a shadow or even of the gunman. Instead another hunk of lead slammed into the dry dust. Helsby scrambled to his feet, and hit the dirt in an alley opposite.

He couldn't see anybody in the street. A third hunk of lead hit the woodwork just above his head. His body tensing up, Helsby looked round the corner again. A shadow flickered in the alley between the buildings opposite. Helsby fired off a barrel.

The dull roar of the shotgun seemed to quieten the air. A couple of seconds later, the people started to come out of the saloons.

'Get inside,' Helsby yelled.

The crowd hesitated.

'Git back inside,' he yelled again.

This time it worked and the crowd started to push their way back inside. The street was quiet again. Everybody had got out of the way. Helsby looked carefully out of the alley. There was no sign of anybody. He slipped into the darkness again, and waited.

'Need any help, Sheriff?' the gunsmith called from over the street.

Helsby figured he must have heard the shooting from his house.

'No, it's OK. Just get out of the street, and find some cover,' Helsby shouted to him.

Helsby moved into the shadows, and waited. The seconds ticked by. He could see nothing from the other alleys, and figured that the fella that was doing the shooting had gone. He moved into the middle of the street, and heard nothing from the alleys. Helsby replaced the spent shells.

The gunsmith came across to join him. 'What was all that about?' he asked.

'Dunno,' Helsby said, still looking up and down the street.

'Maybe it would have somethin' to do with what happened the other night,' the gunsmith said.

Helsby looked at him sharply. 'What would that be?'

'I was in the privy, an' I heard some folks talkin'. Reckon one of them was that Harker woman. The one that came into town with them others to buy the Circle B.'

'Any idea who the other one was?' Helsby asked him.

'Ain't sure. Think it might have been one of them Circle B hands, Gilchrist is his name, but, like I said, I ain't sure.'

'Thanks a heap. Sure would appreciate it if you kept it to yerself,' Helsby said.

'I can do that,' was the answer.

They parted company. The gunsmith went home, Helsby went to his office, and sat in his chair, and took the bottle from the desk and pulled the cork. It sure tasted good. Pushing the cork into the bottle, he put it in the drawer and wiped his mouth with his hand, and thought about the shooting. It could have been Gilchrist, the fella had enough reason to shoot at him. Something about Beth Harker told him she had it in her. Then he remembered the woman who had come in on the stage. Maybe it was her. If she was anywhere, he figured she would be up near Shelby's Hole. He got out of the chair and went outside, and got into the saddle.

He hauled on the reins when he got near Shelby's

Hole. He stopped, and knelt in the same long grass that he had knelt in when he was looking for Grissom. The place was dark and spooky, with no moon to give him any light. The grass snapped as he worked his way towards the cave.

He moved to the cave entrance, and listened. There was no sound. Inch by inch he searched the caves and found nothing. Helsby felt like a fool. He back-tracked to where he had hitched his horse to a tree, and climbed aboard. Gigging it, he headed back to town.

As he reached the edge of town, he heard a set of hoofs coming in his direction. He dragged on the leathers, and waited until the rider had passed him, and took the fork into town. Helsby followed the horse and rider slowly. He could just about see the white tail of the horse. Helsby had expected the horse to be guided into the centre of town, but instead it went across Main Street, and seemed to be heading across town and out again.

The Butterfield Stage Office lay that way, and Helsby knew that there was money kept there overnight. He loosened the leather thong over his gun, but the horse and rider went past the office. Helsby hauled on the leathers as the horse was stopped outside Stone's house. He guided his horse into an alley, and got down.

Cat-footing along the street, he pushed open the gate, and went along the path of Stone's house. He crept to the rear, and looked round. Stone had left the windows open to get the meagre breeze that was easing across his garden.

Inside, he could see Stone and the woman, whose face he could not see, talking quietly. Stone was standing by an empty fireplace, holding a glass of whiskey. The woman was sat in an easy chair, her back to the window. Helsby guessed she was holding a glass as well.

'I couldn't get right in, that sheriff was waiting for me. He followed me out of town. I lost him, and hid up near Shelby's Hole. Then got out just before he got there.'

Stone was doing most of the talking, and doing it quietly, so Helsby couldn't hear what he was saying.

The conversation started to close down, as Stone finished his drink and put the glass on the mantelpiece. He pointed to the door that led to the stairs.

His guest got up as well, and picked up the travelling bag from the floor beside her, and half-turned to the door. Helsby moved quickly away from the window.

His foot caught against the border of the flower bed. Through the window he could see them turning in his direction.

Helsby moved quickly along the path until he reached the end of the house. He stopped and listened. There was no sound coming from the house.

'Musta bin a cat or dog,' Stone said to the woman.

The woman glanced towards the window. 'Bring my horse round and put it in yer stable and check around.'

Stone did as he was told.

'An' if my real nosy neighbours see us. What are they gonna think? Tramping round the garden in the middle of the night: I told you you should have come in on the stage.'

The woman crossed to the window.

'Fer Chris'sake,' Stone said, moving to the window and pulling the curtain across, blocking out what was going on inside. 'You know where your room is,' Stone said, pouring himself another drink.

The woman went up the stairs, and looked into the garden from the back window, and saw Stone taking her horse into the stable. Tossing her bag on the bed, she closed the curtains and started to get undressed.

Helsby got out of Stone's garden. He unhitched his horse, stabled it and went to his office. He figured that the woman he had seen Stone talking to was the woman who had shot Fred Bennet, the woman who had camped out at Shelby's Hole. Now he was going to have to prove it, and tie up all the loose ends.

The way he saw it was Fred Bennet had got the letters from Trenton, and became frightened that his guilty secret would come out, and decided to get out. He had worked for twenty or more years in Red Rock, built up a good-sized ranch, and a good name. If he was going to lose it all, he might have decided to get out, but that didn't explain why the woman Stone was talking to was brought in to kill him. He didn't figure it to be Stone. So it had to be somebody else.

Taking the bottle from the desk, he poured a good measure into a mug and swallowed it. The only other buyers of the Circle B were Beth Harker and her crowd. They looked a better bet than Stone, who was tied up in it somewhere. They were surely a better bet than the Grissom kid.

He locked up and went into the back where he had a bunk. Pulling off his boots, he dropped them on the floor, and fell asleep.

Brett Anderson was going down to see Stone the following morning.

'Hi, Anderson,' Lily Jeffords greeted him as she approached him on the street.

'Hi, yerself,' he said, giving her a smile.

'Yer lookin' in a better mood than the other mornin',' she said. 'Looks like somebody has died an' left you a heap of cash.'

'Had some good news,' he said. 'Betsy Bennet turned up, like she just fell out of Heaven.'

He was glad to see Jeffords' face change colour

as the blood drained out of it.

'Betsy Bennet,' she said hoarsely.

'Betsy Bennet,' he said. 'Came as a real surprise. Me an' Stone put an advert in a couple of newspapers, asking if anybody knew anything about her, and sure enough she turned up. You all right?' he asked her.

'I'm fine,' she answered hoarsely. 'Gotta be goin', Anderson.'

FOURTEEN

She turned and walked in the direction of the
Lucky Lady. Anderson watched her go until she
turned the corner.

Lily walked in through the back way and went
up the stairs to her room. Neither of the other
soiled doves were up, she guessed they were still
sleeping in their rooms. She closed the door
behind her, and opened the drawer of her dressing table. She was glad that Fred had made good.
A shudder ran through her as she remembered
that last night when her old man had taken the
whip to him, leaving the flesh on his back hanging in bloody streaks, and Fred on his knees, his
mouth tight-lipped, without a trace of expression.
Lily, as she had come to think of herself, still
heard her pa raving at Fred taking up with a no-
good whore. She figured that over the years Fred
had gotten used to the beatings, while their
mother and Frank looked on.

Now after all this time someone had come to Red Rock, pretending to be her. Ever since she had seen Anderson with the woman he was introducing as Betsy Bennet, she scoured her memory for her real name. Lily was sure that she knew her, but where from?

Anderson had gone to Stone's office for a meeting with Stone and the others so they could get their story straight. He knew that Helsby was no fool, and he would soon see if something was wrong with their story.

Stone was waiting in his office when Anderson got there. Anderson put his hand in his coat pocket, and put the sheaf of papers on Stone's desk.

'Fred Bennet's will,' he said. 'All signed, sealed, and delivered.'

Beth Harker picked up the papers and looked at them.

'A mite torn and battered,' she said.

'What would you expect if they'd been kept in a ranch house for a while.'

'Guess yer right,' Beth Harker said, grudgingly. 'How long before we can sell the ranch?' she asked him.

'Give or take a couple of weeks,' Anderson said, 'Let folks get to know Betsy, make themselves familiar with her. Then we, or at least Betsy, can sell the ranch and the land. Then we can go our separate ways.'

Beth and Dan Harker looked relieved. The Davenports shared their look.

'Be glad to see the back of this part of the country,' Dan Harker said.

The others nodded, except Mary Dillon.

'When do I git my cut?' she asked them.

Beth Harker gave her a hard look, and thought that Mary Dillon might give them some trouble.

'Real soon, honey,' Anderson said, going over to her and putting his arms on her shoulders. She squirmed away quickly, her face turning red.

'That's enough, Anderson. I've told you before to keep yer paws to yerself,' she snarled at him.

Anderson backed off, an angry look crossing his face. 'Sure thing. Say four weeks.'

'Ain't you got that kinda money here now? I don't want to walk away from this empty-handed.'

'You've already had some,' Anderson said. 'You'll get the rest when we've sold the ranch.'

'I hope so,' Mary Dillon said, edging to the door. 'Or Sheriff Helsby might be interested in what I've got to tell him.'

Beth Harker and Anderson exchanged glances.

'We'll work it out, honey,' Anderson said reassuringly.

'You'd better. I've bin round fellas since I knew what a fella was for. I know just what you're like. I'm gonna get myself somethin' to eat.'

Mary Dillon went out of the office leaving

everybody to their own thoughts.

Beth Harker was the first to speak. 'Seems like we're gonna have to take care of her,' she said, looking at the others in turn.

Mary Dillon walked out into the dusty street, and headed across to Stoop's café.

There were a few people in there, and one of them was Lily Jeffords.

As she came away from the counter holding a tray with a breakfast on it Lily caught her arm.

'You got some kinda problem?' Mary Dillon asked her.

Lily smiled up at her.

'Just wanted to welcome you to Red Rock. Sit down, won't you?' she said, tightening her grip on Mary's arm.

'Sure, I can spare you some time,' Mary said as she sat down, and put her tray on the table.

'Glad to hear it,' Lily said. 'Betsy Bennet, ain't it?' she said smoothly.

'You're a sharp one. Betsy Bennet it is.'

'I can't quite place you, but I don't seem to recall you using the handle Betsy,' Lily said to her, leaning across the table.

'You got me mixed up with some other gal,' Mary said nervously, as she began to stir her coffee.

'I don't think so,' Lily Jeffords said, giving her a hard look. 'We knew each other a few years back.'

'We ain't met,' Mary said.

Lily shrugged. 'Maybe I was mistaken. So, you come to claim yer inheritance? Must be quite a sum. The ranch, an' whatever Fred had in the bank fer a rainy day.'

'I come to claim my inheritance. You make it sound like I was doin' somethin' wrong,' Mary said, watching Lily's face.

Lily got up from the table, and left the café. Mary Dillon watched her go. It had been her plan to make a fresh start with the money Anderson would give her, now it looked like that might go wrong. Maybe she should tell Anderson right off.

'Didn't expect to see you so soon,' Anderson said when Mary Dillon returned to his office.

'You might have to change your plans,' she said quickly.

'What do you mean by that? You gettin' cold feet on us,' he said, leaning across the desk.

'No, I ain't gettin' cold feet,' she snapped at him. 'But I figure Lily Jeffords could be steppin' on our toes.'

Anderson looked at her. 'What d'you mean by that?'

'I mean I think she knows I'm not Betsy Bennet,' she said. 'I thought I recognized her on the street. Then when I saw her in the café after I left you an' the others, she as good told me I was a liar. She didn't come right out an' say it, but

136

that's what she was gettin' at.'

'Damn,' Anderson scorched the air. 'That's the last thing we wanted.'

'I ain't too pleased either,' Mary Dillon snapped. 'It was yours an' Stone's plan, so you an' Stone had better get it fixed up,' she snarled.

Inwardly Anderson fumed. There had been months of planning since Beth Harker came to him with the scheme; a scheme which she had pulled off in Montana Territory.

'Damn it,' he ground out again.

'If that's all you can come up with, we'd better go across an' see Helsby now,' Mary Dillon said.

Anderson wanted to slap her when she said this. Instead, he held his temper and thought.

'I'll go across an' see Beth when you've gone,' he said.

'Don't leave it too long,' Mary Dillon told him, getting to her feet.

Anderson watched her go, gave her a few minutes, then went to see Beth Harker.

'Lily Jeffords knows Betsy Bennet,' she almost howled, when Anderson told her.

'What are we gonna do?' her husband whined, the thought of a rope coming into his mind.

'We ain't going to start panicking,' Beth Harker said, handing him a bottle and glass from the table.

'I think we should get our friend to sort out the mess,' she said to Anderson. 'You get hold of

Stone and tell him to get over here.'

'OK,' Anderson said.

Lily Jeffords was in her room thinking about Mary Dillon, and where she knew her from. It was like she told her, it had been a while ago. Taking the lipstick from her bag, she put it to her lips, and glanced into the mirror to see that she was aiming for the right place. It came to her where she had known Mary Dillon from.

She had come into the cathouse in Dodge where Lily had been working, looking for work as a soiled dove. Lily's boss, a Frenchman who wore a patch over one eye, had told her that Mary Dillon had been an actress, who just couldn't act. Lily hadn't got to know her well. Mary Dillon kept herself to herself when she wasn't working.

Then, one day, she just up and walked out of the place, along with a thousand dollars of One Eye's money. Lily hadn't seen her from that day until the day she came in to collect Betsy's inheritance.

She would have to tell Helsby. Then it crossed her mind that she might have something to do with Fred's murder. She got up, and went down to see Helsby.

'Yeah, Lily,' he said when she came in.

Lily sat herself down across from Helsby.

'This Betsy, she ain't who she says she is.'

138

Helsby said nothing for a second, then, 'Yeah, I know.'

Lily watched him. 'You got anythin' else to say right now?'

'No. I'm just gonna have to wait,' he said after a minute.

'What fer?' she asked him.

'There's a heap of other things happenin', an' I don't want to spoil everything,' he said quietly. 'Now, you leave it up to me, an' I'll get it sorted out. Yer just gonna have to trust me.'

Lily didn't like the idea too much, but if that was the way Helsby wanted to play, that was up to him.

She left his office, and went over to the saloon. Stone was on the veranda. He tipped his hat to her.

'Mornin', Lily,' he said affably.

'Mornin', Mayor,' Lily replied.

'Yer lookin' in a fine state of health,' he said to her.

'Thanks, Mayor. Yer not lookin' too bad yerself. I've bin talkin' to Betsy Bennet. She seems a nice gal.'

'I know,' Stone told her. 'Turned up at the right time,' he said.

'The luck of the thing,' Lily replied. 'Anyway, it's bin nice talkin' to you, Stone, but I've got things to do.'

'Bin nice talkin' to you, Lily,' Stone replied,

touching the brim of his hat as Lily turned and walked into the saloon.

Stone walked across the street to the general store where a middle-aged woman about Lily's height was standing pretending to look into the shop window.

'Git a good look at her?' he asked the woman, as they turned and walked towards his house.

'Good enough,' was the answer. 'I'll figure out a plan later. Just tell me all you know about her.' Her voice was quiet, and silky, with a touch of malice in it.

Stone let them in, and went into the kitchen to fix up some coffee while the woman went upstairs to work on her plan. When he had boiled up the coffee, he took a cup upstairs, and knocked on the bedroom door.

'Come in,' was the answer.

Stone opened the door and went inside. His face must have shown what he was thinking. The woman had been wearing a plain black dress, now she had changed into something more feminine.

'Just leave the cup on the table. I can see from yer face what yer thinking. Forget it. This is a business deal. I was never interested in that sort of thing, so don't try anything or I'll kill you.'

Stone put the cup on the table and went downstairs again.

The woman sat on the chair facing the window. The light was going, but she kept the curtains open. Slowly, she drank the coffee, and thought about Lily Jeffords.

It shouldn't be hard to kill her, she thought. No harder than killing the owner of the Circle B. Stone and the others had given her a list of his comings and goings, and she just took her pick. One shot up-close, and that had been it. Pity about having to leave the empty case on the ground. She always made a practice of taking the spent cartridge cases with her, but she had thought that she had heard somebody coming up the trail, and there was nothing more certain to get you hanged than a dead body, and a smoking gun. So she had crept away from the scene, leaving the spent case in amongst the grass. The following morning, she had ridden to Aurelia, and caught a train back east.

She turned her thoughts to Lily Jeffords, and took a drink from the cup. Lily Jeffords seldom left the saloon. She had no friends outside the other two soiled doves. She never seemed to leave the town limits. The woman leaned back in her chair, stretched her supple body, then took another drink from the coffee cup.

If Lily Jeffords wouldn't come out of town, she would have to figure a way to get her out. The one thing she wasn't going to do was to go into the saloon and shoot her there. No, she had to figure a way to get her where she could get a clean shot at her, and have a way out. She drank the coffee, and closed the curtains.

Stone was at the breakfast table when she got down there the next morning. Stone looked her up, and down, in spite of what she had said to him.

'Lily Jeffords,' she began.

Stone looked across the table at her. 'What about her?'

'I saw her talking to this woman you've got lined up to play Betsy. From the way they were talking, Betsy seemed to know her, or at least that's the impression I got.'

'Yeah,' Stone replied, buttering a piece of toast.

'Here's what we do,' the woman replied, filling up a cup with coffee.

'Tell Lily Jeffords that Betsy wants to see her. Then just get me the place and the time, and make sure you are where folks can see you.'

'OK,' Stone said. 'I'll get right on it.'

When Stone had finished up his breakfast he left his house, and went down to the saloon. When he had left the house, the assassin went upstairs, and took the travelling bag from under the bed. She snapped the lock, and pushed the clothes aside.

Beneath them was a rifle that could be broken down, along with a box of bullets that she had made back in New York. Methodically, she cleaned each part of the gun, then inspected each of the shells. Satisfied, she put everything back in the bag, covered them with her clothes, and pushed the bag under the bed.

'What are you sayin'?' Lily Jeffords asked Stone.

Her mouth was dry from the redeye she had been drinking the night before, and her head buzzed. She looked at Stone through bloodshot eyes.

'I'm sayin' Betsy Bennet's bin to see me. She reckons you got off on the wrong foot, an' she wants to put things right with you.'

Lily started listening to what the mayor had to say.

'She wants to meet you, try an' sort somethin' out.'

'Any idea what she's got in mind?'

'No. She wants to figure it out with you. I reckon it's something to do with both yer pasts.'

'OK,' the whore said. 'Go ahead an' fix somethin' up.'

Stone felt relieved. For a minute it had looked like Lily wasn't going to go for it.

'Just tell me what you got in mind,' Lily said, reaching for the mug of coffee that Stone had brought up with him.

'You know the old line cabin on the Lazy G land?'

'Sure I know it.' She had brought the Grissom kid into town from there. 'Meet her at six this evenin',' Stone said.

'Six it is,' Lily replied.

Stone got up, and made for the door.

'One other thing,' Lily said, finishing the coffee.

Stone wondered what was coming next.

'Next time. No sugar,' she said, holding up the cup.

Stone laughed drily, and went down to fix up his alibi. When he had gone, Lily didn't know who to be suspicious of. Betsy Bennet or Stone, but something sure was wrong. Maybe she should have a word with Helsby.

'Yer out bright an' early,' Helsby said to Lily when he saw her coming out of the saloon.

'I need to talk to you, Helsby.'

'Somethin' the matter?'

'Ain't rightly sure. We'd better go over to yer office.'

They walked across the street.

'What is it?'

'Stone. I ain't rightly sure, but he's up to somethin,' she began.

'Stone's always up to somethin,' Helsby told her.

'Yeah, but this time it's different. He wants me to go out to the old line cabin where I hid Grissom. He wants me to meet with Betsy.'

'What's wrong with that?' Helsby asked her.

'This Betsy ain't who she says she is,' Lily said.

'I think you've said this before. How do you know she ain't who she says she is?'

'Look, Helsby, give me a break an' just trust me.'

Helsby watched her face for a minute. 'OK. What do you want me to do?'

'I ain't rightly sure. Just ride out to the cabin some ways behind me, an' keep an eye on things.'

'OK,' Helsby said. 'I'll follow you up to the cabin.'

'Thanks,' Lily said.

They arranged for Lily to leave at five, and Helsby would follow her up fifteen minutes later, and keep her in sight.

The day dragged with Lily getting more and more worried. In his office, Helsby checked his six-gun. Lily, feeling apprehensive, saddled up her horse, and climbed aboard. Stone gave her a friendly wave as she rode out.

When she was out of sight, he walked down to Anderson's office. Helsby watched him go into Anderson's place, then walked over to the livery and got his own horse, and followed Lily. He saw her, and eased off on the pace of his horse. Helsby was lucky; the ground about here was heavily wooded, so he didn't have a lot of trouble keeping out of sight. He caught occasional glimpses of her between the trees and rocks.

FIFTEEN

The assassin saw Lily emerge from the trees. In a leisurely way, she raised the rifle to her shoulder, and decided to give her a little more time to get closer to the cabin. Lily came on, the leathers slippery in her hand. Letting go of them with one hand, she wiped them on her skirt.

The assassin beaded Lily in her sights, and started to squeeze the trigger, going for a head-shot. As she applied the last ounce of pressure, the leathers, wet with sweat, slipped out of Lily's grasp. Leaning down to retrieve them, she heard the shot and felt the air part over her head.

Helsby heard the shot as he got to the edge of the trees. He reined in his horse, and jumped out of the saddle. Lily was lying on the ground. Helsby could see no sign of life. Her horse had galloped to the cabin and was waiting, chewing at the grass.

There was no sign of the assassin who had fired

the shot. Helsby waited. Flies started to gather over Lily's body. Whoever was in there was in no rush to come out. Inside, the assassin waited. She hadn't seen Helsby, but she was taking no chances.

Lily Jeffords lay dazed in the grass, the hot sun beating down on her face and the flies starting to take an interest in the blood that ran from her hairline down the exposed side of her face. She blinked in the sun as the long grass came into focus. Where the hell was Helsby? Just like a fella to be late.

Helsby watched from the cover of the brush. Lily hadn't moved, so he figured she was dead.

The assassin took a step towards the window, and took a quick glance out. Helsby saw her, and unshipped his Winchester. He levered a round into the chamber, and waited. There was a movement inside the cabin. Quickly, he raised the Winchester to his cheek. He saw the movement again, and lined up the Winchester, then squeezed the trigger. The Winchester bucked against his shoulder, and the flame sprouted, just as the assassin saw the movemement. She died straight away, as the piece of lead struck her between the eyes.

She fell back against the crate that Grissom had sat on. Helsby threw a look at the cabin, and waited. He moved slowly through the long grass towards the cabin, giving the window a wide berth. He tried to see where Lily was, but the grass was getting in his way. He crouched down by the side of the cabin, and checked the front. Cautiously, he worked his way round to the back and found the door.

Behind him a bird screeched in a tree, and soared upwards. Helsby spun round and dropped to one knee, the Winchester coming up to his shoulder. He just stopped himself squeezing the trigger.

He turned to face the door. It looked like it was going to fall apart. Bracing himself, Helsby gave it a kick. There was a shower of dust, and the splintered door smashed and fell inwards. Helsby jumped to one side, half expecting a shot. When it didn't come, he took a look inside. He could just make out a body. Helsby kicked some of the door out of the way. The bits splintered and cracked under his feet.

For a moment he stood dumbfounded as he looked down at the woman's face. He reckoned she would have been a looker, if the bullet that had ploughed into her skull hadn't mashed up her face. He knelt beside her, his long shadow covering her face again. Tenderly, he closed her eyes and stood up. If he had been a religious man, he would have mumbled a prayer, but Bill Thompson had put an end to that.

Picking up the shell case he put it in his vest pocket, and went round to the front of the cabin.

The first thing he saw was Lily Jeffords staggering around in the waist-high grass, her head bleeding.

The sheriff ran through the grass to catch her before she fell. He picked her up and carried her into the cabin. He laid her on the floor. Gently, he slapped her face until the colour came back, and she opened her eyes.

'Best not look over there,' he said.

'You got him?' Lily Jeffords asked.

'Got her,' Helsby said to her.

Lily pushed him out of the way and struggled into a sitting position.

'Any idea who she is?' she asked Helsby.

Helsby shook his head. 'No, but I figure Stone would, or somebody close to him.'

'You mean Anderson?' Lily threw a look in the assassin's direction.

'Maybe, an' maybe a couple of others. I think I'm starting' to see the light,' Helsby said, taking the makings out, and handing them to Lily.

'Thanks,' she said when she had built her own. 'Now, if you don't mind, Helsby, let's git outside, so we can smoke in peace with nobody to spy on us.'

They took the smokes outside.

'So what are you goin' to do?' she asked him.

'I'm gonna take you back over yer saddle,' he said lightly.

Lily gave him an alarmed look.

149

'Then I'm gonna come right back out here to see who shows up. Git yer horse.'

They rode back to Red Rock. Helsby hauled on the reins, and dismounted.

'It's gonna be pretty uncomfortable for a spell, Lil,' he said. 'If you'd care to get across the saddle, we'll git into Doc Lennon's office.'

It was just getting dark when Helsby hauled up outside the doc's office. The light was still on in the front room. Helsby went in and found the doc, pulling the top down on his desk.

'Hi, Sheriff,' he said pulling off his glasses. 'Something wrong?'

'Need a hand gettin' a body in here, an' I don't want you makin' a big fuss about it.'

'Anythin' you say,' Doc Lennon said in a puzzled way.

Between them, they got Lily into the office.

'Put her on the couch,' Doc Lennon said.

'Ain't no need fer that,' Lily said, getting up.

'What's goin' on?' the startled doc said.

'Tell you later when I get back,' Helsby said as he went out.

From the front door, he took a quick look up and down the street. There was nobody around. Climbing into the saddle he rode back to the line shack.

Stone had waited into the evening, and was starting to get worried when his hired gun hadn't got back. Angrily, he stalked round to his stable, and saddled his horse.

Lily walked out of the doc's office shortly after Stone had gone. She walked across to the saloon, and up to her room. The other girls were down in the saloon.

Digging a bottle of redeye from her dressing table, she pulled the cork, and put the bottle to her lips, and tilted her head back. The raw spirit burned her throat. She put the bottle down, and coughed a while. When she felt better, she picked the bottle up again.

'Here's to you, Fred.' She took another long drink, then stood and put the bottle away.

For a while she rummaged round in the drawer until she found what she was looking for.

'Have you seen Mary Dillon?' she asked the head barman.

'Yeah, I saw her headin' back to the hotel after she'd bin over to see Anderson.'

'Thanks,' Lily said and headed that way.

When Mary Dillon opened the door, and saw Lily, a couple of expressions came over her face.

'What do you want?' she asked Lily.

'A quiet word with you,' Lily told her, walking into the room.

'Hey, this is my room, what do you think yer doing?'

'Like I said, I want a word with you,' Lily said

sharply, pulling the gun from her bag.

'What is this?' Mary Dillon said, her voice rising with fear.

'This li'l bitty thing is my brother's gun. The first gun he had. My pa gave it him. If my brother had had it in his belt when Pa lashed him, my brother would have killed him.'

'So just who is this brother of yours?' Mary Dillon asked Lily.

'Fred Bennet,' Lily said.

Mary Dillon's face turned white; her eyes became full of tears as Lily drew back the hammer.

'Don't kill me,' she whimpered. 'Please don't kill me.'

Lily felt herself relax. She was glad that it hadn't come to it.

'Just tell me everythin', then we can go an' see Helsby. He'll see you get a fair shake, which is more than Fred got.'

'I don't know all that much. Anderson came up to Aurelia to see me. Stone, your mayor, wasn't payin' fer what he was gettin'.'

'Keep talkin,' Lily said.

'An' they came up with a scheme, along with that couple that I've bin seein' a lot of.'

'An' that scheme meant killin' Fred, an' stealin' his land,' Lily's face had flared up. 'You murderin'—' She bit the rest off.

Mary Dillon had gone white, and she felt

certain that Lily was going to kill her.

'Git on yer feet so we can have a little talk with Helsby,' Lily told her, pointing the gun in the direction of the door.

Mary Dillon got up slowly from the settee, a feeling of disappointment in her stomach. She had been so close to getting the one big score she needed.

'Helsby back yet?' she asked Jenny when she saw her approaching the jail.

'No,' Jenny said, eyeing Mary Dillon curiously. 'If you want to lock her up, yer gonna have to find some place else.'

Lily thought, then said to Mary, 'I know.'

She took Mary Dillon down to Doc Lennon's.

'Just bring her in,' he said.

'Got some rope or somethin'? I'd feel better if she was tied up.'

'Sure,' the doc said, and went to get some.

Helsby had headed right back to the line cabin. Dismounting, he tethered his horse to some scrub behind it. He moved the assassin's body out of the cabin, and covered it with his horse blanket and went inside to wait and see who turned up.

The cabin loomed on the skyline as Stone approached it. He hauled up for a few minutes to let his stomach settle before pressing on the rest of the way. Helsby heard the drumbeat of hoofs, and stood up behind the door.

The hoofs stopped outside, and he heard the jingle of spurs as the rider got down. Drawing his .45, he waited, his own heart beating, half expecting Bill Thompson to come through the door. His mouth went dry, and he felt the urge for a drop of redeye, to settle him down, then the door opened, and he reached down to turn up the lamp.

Stone jumped back, taken by surprise.

'Hi, Stone,' Helsby said quietly. 'What are you doin' up here?'

Stone's heart skipped a beat.

'What are you doin' here, Helsby?' he asked, his mouth dry.

'Fair's fair, Mayor. I asked first.'

Stone struggled for an answer, then panicked, and tried for the door. Helsby crossed the room in a couple of strides, and caught Stone by the back of the neck, and dragged him across the room and slammed him against the wall. He heard the air come out of Stone's lungs with a whoosh. Letting go of the mayor, he stood there while Stone slid to the floor. He grabbed Stone by the shirt front, and hauled him to his feet.

'Let's have it, Stone, an' I mean the truth. I've guessed most of it, just fill me in on the details.'

'What do you want to know?' an ashen-faced Stone asked him.

'Those newcomers in town, they fixed it to have Fred murdered, an' I guess Anderson would fix up the sale of the land, an' the rest of the stuff. If you don't confirm what I said, that woman would do it to save her own neck,' he lied.

'She'll never say anything,' Stone said.

'She would if she could save her own neck,' Helsby lied again.

'Maybe I could get the same deal,' Stone said, clutching at straws.

'Maybe you could,' Helsby told him. 'Now git over here, an' sit down.'

When Stone had sat down, Helsby took a wad of paper and a pencil out of his trouser pocket, and put them in front of Stone.

'Start writing,' he said.

His hand shaking, Stone started to write. Helsby watched him in silence.

'You about finished?' Helsby asked after a while.

Stone nodded, and handed the paper to Helsby. He read it slowly then folded it up, and put it in his trouser pocket.

'Let's get back to Red Rock,' Helsby said, taking the ashen-faced mayor out to the back where he had tethered his horse. He then took him round the front of the cabin where the mayor's horse waited patiently.

When they got back to Red Rock, Helsby hauled up outside his office, climbed down, then pulled Stone out of the saddle, and pushed him inside.

Lily came to meet them. 'I'll get Mary Dillon, she's down at the doc's.'

She came back with Mary Dillon when Helsby had just locked up Stone.

'Take it easy, Lily,' Helsby said. 'The mayor signed a confession.'

'Wait up. Mary's told me what's bin goin' on.'

She told Helsby what had happened.

'Thanks, Lily,' Helsby said. 'Stay here an' keep an eye on these two.'

'Yeah, we'll be just fine,' Lily said. 'Won't we, Mr Mayor?'

Stone said nothing.

Helsby stood on the veranda for a minute or two, then headed in the direction of the hotel where the Harker's were staying.

From behind the curtains in the room, Beth Harker watched Helsby cross the dusty street, his right hand hanging loosely by his gun. She knew why he was coming.

Her body went cold at the thought of losing the money from the sale of the ranch and the land. She knew that if she was caught she would hang, along with the others, not that she cared about them.

Wearily, she walked back to the bedroom where her husband lay snoring on the bed with a single sheet covering his corpulent body. He moved restlessly as she passed into the next room, and took the small pistol from her handbag. Sitting down, she spun the chamber and put it to her head. From outside Helsby and the night clerk heard the shot.

'Stand back,' Helsby ordered the clerk.

He got out of Helsby's way. Helsby's boot smashed the door in. He rushed into the room. 'She's dead,' he told the clerk. 'Go an' git Doc Lennon.'

The clerk rushed down the corridor and into the street, brushing past Moran. As he did so, Moran grabbed his arm, and pulled him back.

'What's yer hurry?' he demanded of the clerk.

'Sheriff's sent me for the doc. There's bin a shootin' in the Harkers' room,' he gabbled, then pulled away from Moran, and headed for the doc's.

Moran watched him go, then went into the hotel, and up the stairs. At the top of the landing, he stopped, and waited. Helsby came out of the room, and looked up and down the corridor. Moran drew his gun, and fired. The shot whipped past Helsby's head. Helsby hit the floor, and twisted as he did so. His gun came into his hand, and he heard the floorboards creak at the top of the landing. Moran showed himself just long enough for Helsby to put a piece of lead into his hide.

Moran reeled and fell down the stairs as the first of the room doors opened. People ran out

157

onto the landing in their nightclothes demanding to know what was going on. Helsby ushered them back into their rooms, then noticed the Harkers' accomplices standing looking fearful in the corridor.

'Best get back inside,' he said, following them in.

'What's happened?' Sarah Davenport asked him.

'There's bin a shootin',' Helsby told them.

They backed into the room.

'What's been goin' on?'

'Yer boss is dead. That's if she was the boss. You ain't got the brains or the balls fer it,' Helsby told them. 'An' I got a confession from Stone. So all I got to do is round up Anderson. Git dressed, an' we'll go down to the jail.'

The pair went into the bedroom, and started to get dressed. Helsby sat in one of the chairs, and rolled himself a stogie. He had almost finished when there was a knock at the door. He put the stogie on the table got up and drew his .45.

'Yeah, who is it?' he demanded, cocking the .45.

'Me. Doc Lennon. I hear you've got some business for me,' the doc said.

'Yeah, come in.'

The doc looked at Helsby. 'Where is it?'

'Room next door,' Helsby told him. 'It's Beth Harker. Only got a quick look. I think she shot herself.'

'I'll go an' take a look,' Doc Lennon said.

When he had gone, Helsby put a lucifer to the end of his stogie.

'You folks about ready?'

There was a mumble from inside the room, and they came out.

'Let's go,' Helsby said.

They filed out onto the landing. Moran's body was still there, his eyes staring up at the ceiling. There were some folks out in the corridor watching the procession curiously as it went down the stairs, and out into the street. At the jail, Helsby locked them up.

'That just leaves Anderson,' he said to Lily.

'He's still in his office. I saw the light when I was bringin' Mary in. Though I can't see what he's doin there at this time of the night. Say, where are you goin'?'

Helsby ran down the street and across town. He stopped by the window of Anderson's office. He could see that a lamp was on in the back. Curiously, he turned the handle, and felt it give. He pushed it open, and drew his gun. Helsby cat footed in the direction of the door. He stopped, and listened. He could hear nothing.

Anderson turned, his face a mask of surprise.

'Don't move, Anderson,' the sheriff snarled at him.

'Relax, Helsby,' he said smoothly, getting to his feet.

'Step away from the stove,' Helsby told him. 'An' face the wall.'

When Anderson had done this, Helsby picked up some of the papers that Anderson had been trying to burn.

'Seems like there's enough here to get you into a heap of trouble,' Helsby said.

Anderson said nothing as Helsby pushed him through the door.

By the time he got Anderson locked up, the jail was pretty full.

'Lily,' he said to the whore. 'Would you care to get down to Anderson's office and pick up any papers that it looked like he was going to burn.'

'Gotcha,' Lily said.

Wearily, Helsby sat down behind his desk. It sure seemed to have been a long day. He reached into the drawer, and took out the bottle, and pulled the cork.

'That's gettin' to be a habit,' Jenny said from the door.

Helsby looked up. 'What are you doin' down here?' he asked her, more sharply than he had intended.

'Heard a lot of commotion, so I thought I'd come down, an' see what's been goin' on.'

'I cleaned up the Fred Bennet killing.'

'You gonna tell me about it?' she asked him.

'It's complicated, an' I'm tired. I'll tell you in the mornin' an' maybe I'll tell you about yer pa.'